Alexis
cool
as a
cupcake

SIMON SPOTLIGHT
An imprint of Simon & Schuster Children's Publishing Division
1230 Avenue of the Americas, New York, New York 10020
Copyright © 2012 by Simon & Schuster, Inc. All rights reserved, including the right of reproduction in whole or in part in any form.
SIMON SPOTLIGHT and colophon are registered trademarks of Simon & Schuster, Inc.
Text by Elizabeth Doyle Carey
Chapter header illustrations by Ana Benaroya
Designed by Laura Roode
For information about special discounts for bulk purchases, please contact Simon & Schuster Special Sales at 1-866-506-1949 or business@simonandschuster.com.
Manufactured in the United States of America 1219 OFF
First Edition
6 8 10 9 7
ISBN 978-1-4424-5080-6
ISBN 978-1-4424-5081-3 (eBook)
Library of Congress Catalog Card Number 2012933803

CUPCAKE DIARIES

Alexis
cool
as a
cupcake

by coco simon

Simon Spotlight
New York   London   Toronto   Sydney   New Delhi

CHAPTER 1

Partners? What Partners?

*B*usiness first. That's one of my mottoes.

When my best friends and I get together to discuss our cupcake company, the Cupcake Club, I am all about business. My name is Alexis Becker, and I am the business planner of the group. This means I kind of take care of everything—pricing, scheduling, and ingredient inventory—the nuts and bolts of it all. So when we actually go to make the cupcakes and sell them, we're all set.

Mia Vélaz-Cruz is our fashion-forward, stylish person, who is great at presentation and coming up with really good ideas, and Katie Brown and Emma Taylor are real bakers, so they have lots of ideas on ingredients and how things should taste. Together we make a great team.

But today, when we were having our weekly meeting at Mia's house, they would not let me do my job. It was so frustrating!

I had out the leather-bound accounts ledger that Mia's mom gave me, and I was going through all our costs and all the money that's owed to us, when Mia interrupted.

"Ooh! I forgot to tell you I had an idea for your costume for the pep rally parade, Katie!" said Mia enthusiastically, as if I wasn't in the middle of reading out columns of numbers for the past two jobs we've had. The high school in our town holds a huge parade and pep rally right before school starts. It's a pretty big deal. One year some kids decided to dress up in costumes for the parade, and now everybody dresses up. The local newspaper sends reporters, and there are usually pictures of it on the first page of the paper the very next day.

"Oh good, what is it?" asked Katie, as if she was thrilled for the interruption.

"Ahem," I said. "Are we conducting business here or having a coffee klatch?" That's what our favorite science teacher, Ms. Biddle, said when we whispered in class. Apparently, a coffee klatch is something gossipy old ladies do: drink coffee and chatter mindlessly.

"Yeah, c'mon, guys. Let's get through this," said Emma. I know she was trying to be supportive of me, but "get through this"? As if they just had to listen to me before they got to the fun stuff? That was kind of insulting!

"I'm not reading this stuff for my own health, you know," I said. I knew I sounded really huffy, but I didn't care. I do way more behind-the-scenes work than anyone else in this club, and I don't think they have any idea how much time and effort it takes. Now, I *do* love it, but everyone has a limit, and I have almost reached mine.

"Sorry, Alexis! I just was spacing out and it crossed my mind," admitted Mia. It was kind of a lame apology, since she was admitting she was spacing out during my presentation.

"Whatever," I said. "Do you want to listen or should I just forget about it?"

"No, no, we're listening!" protested Katie. "Go on!" But I caught her winking and nodding at Mia as Mia nodded and gestured to her.

I shut the ledger. "Anyway, that's all," I said.

Mia and Katie were so engrossed in their sign language that they didn't even realize I'd cut it short. Emma seemed relieved and didn't protest.

So that's how it's going to be, I thought. *Then*

fine! I'd just do the books and buy the supplies and do all the scheduling and keep it to myself. No need to involve the whole club, anyway. I folded my arms across my chest and waited for someone to speak. But of course, it wasn't about business.

"Well?" asked Katie.

"Okay, I was thinking, what about a genie? And you can get George Martinez to be an astronaut. Then you can wear something really dreamy and floaty and magical, like on that old TV show *I Dream of Jeannie* that's on Boomerang?" Mia was smiling with pride at her idea.

"Ooooh! I love that idea!" squealed Katie. "But how do I get George to be an astronaut?" She propped her chin on her hand and frowned.

"Wait!" interrupted Emma. "Why would George Martinez need to be an astronaut?"

Mia looked at her like she was crazy. "Because a *boy* has to be your partner for the parade. You know that!"

Emma flushed a deep red. "No, I did not know that. Who told you that?"

I felt a pit growing in my stomach. Even though I was mad and trying to stay out of this annoying conversation, the news stunned me too, and I couldn't remain silent. "Yeah, who told you that?" I repeated.

Mia and Katie shrugged and looked at each other, then back at us.

"Um, I don't know," said Katie. "It's just common knowledge?"

I found this annoying since it was our first real pep rally and this was major news. "No, it is *not* common knowledge." I glared at Mia.

"Sorry," said Mia sheepishly.

I pressed my lips together. Then I said, "Well? Who are *you* going with?"

Mia looked away. "I haven't really made up my mind," she said.

"Do you have lots of choices?" I asked. I was half annoyed and half jealous. Mia is really pretty and stylish and not that nervous around boys.

She laughed a little. "Not exactly. But Katie does!"

Emma and I looked at each other, like, *How could we have been so clueless?*

"Stop!" Katie laughed, turning beet red again.

"Well, 'fess up! Who are they?" I asked.

Katie rolled her eyes. "Oh, I don't know."

Mia began ticking off names on her fingers. "George Martinez always teases her when he sees her, which we all know means he likes her. He even mentioned something about the parade and asked Katie what her costume was going to be, right?"

Katie nodded.

Mia continued, "And then there's Joe Fraser. Another possibility."

"Stop!" protested Katie. "That's all. This is too mortifying! Let's change the subject to something boring, like Cupcake revenue!"

"Thanks a lot!" I said. I was hurt that she said it because I don't find Cupcake revenue boring. I find it fascinating. I love to think of new ways to make money.

How do my best friends and I have such different interests? I wondered.

"Sorry, but you know what I mean," said Katie. "It stresses me out to talk about who likes whom."

Still.

"Well, no one likes me!" said Emma.

"That's not true. I'm sure people like you," said Mia. But I noticed she didn't try to list anyone.

"What do we do if we don't have a boy to go with?" I asked.

"Well, girls could go with their girl friends, but no one really does that. I think it's just kind of dorky. . . ."

I felt a flash of annoyance. Since when was Mia such a know-it-all about the pep rally and what was done and what wasn't and what was dorky and what wasn't?

"I guess I could go with Matt . . . ," said Emma, kind of thinking out loud.

"What?!" I couldn't contain my surprise. Emma knows I have a crush on her older brother, and in the back of my mind, throughout this whole conversation, I'd been trying to think if I'd have the nerve to ask him. Not that I'd ever ask if he'd do matchy-matchy costumes with me, but just to walk in the parade together. After all, he *had* asked me to dance at my sister's sweet sixteen party.

Emma looked at me. "What?"

I didn't want to admit I'd been thinking that *I'd* ask him, so I said the next thing I could think of. "You'd go with your brother? Isn't *that* kind of dorky?" I felt mean saying it, but I was annoyed.

Emma winced, and I felt a little bad.

But Mia shook her head. "No, not if your brother is older and is cool, like Matt; it's not dorky."

Oh great. Now she'd just given Emma free rein to ask Matt and I had no one! "You know what? I'm going to check with Dylan on all this," I said.

7

My older sister would certainly know all the details of how this should be done. And she was definitely not dorky.

There was an uncomfortable silence. Finally, I said, "Look, we don't have to worry about all this right now, so let's just get back to business, okay?" And at last they were eager to discuss my favorite subject, if only because the other topics had turned out to be so stressful for us.

I cleared my throat and read from my notebook. "We have Jake's best friend Max's party, and Max's mom wants something like what we did for Jake. . . ." We'd made Jake Cakes—dirt with worms cupcakes made out of crushed Oreos and gummy worms for Emma's little brother's party, and they were a huge hit.

"Right," said Emma, nodding. "I was thinking maybe we could do Mud Pies?"

"Excellent. Let's think about what we need for the ingredients. There's—"

"Sorry to interrupt, but . . ."

We all looked at Katie.

"Just one more tiny question? Do you think Joe Fraser is a little bit cooler than George Martinez?"

I stared at her coldly. "What does that have to do with Mud Pies?"

"Sorry," said Katie, shrugging. "I was just wondering."

"Anyway, Mud Pie ingredients are . . ."

We brainstormed, uninterrupted, for another five minutes and got a list of things kind of organized for a Mud Pie proposal and sample baking session. Then we turned to our next big job, baking cupcakes for a regional swim meet fund-raiser.

Mia had been absentmindedly sketching in her notebook, and now she looked up. "I have a great idea for what we could do for the cupcakes for the swim meet!"

"Oh, let's see!" I said, assuming she'd sketched it out. I peeked over her shoulder, expecting to see a cupcake drawing, and instead there was a drawing of a glamorous witch costume, like something out of *Wicked*.

"Oh," I said. Here I'd been thinking we were all engaged in the cupcake topic, and it turned out Mia had been still thinking about the pep rally parade all along.

"Sorry," she said. "But I was *thinking* about cupcakes."

"Whatever," I said. I tossed my pen down on the table and closed my notebook. "This meeting is adjourned."

"Come on, Alexis," said Mia. "It's not that big a deal."

"Yeah, all work and no play makes for a bad day, boss lady!" added Katie.

"I am *not* the boss lady!" I said. I was mad and hurt. "I don't want to be the boss lady. In fact, I am not any kind of boss. Not anymore! You guys can figure this all out on your own."

I stood up and quickly gathered my things into my bag.

"Hey, Alexis, please! We aren't trying to be mean, we're just distracted!" said Mia.

"You guys think this is all a joke! If I didn't hustle everything along and keep track, nothing would get done!" I said, swinging my bag up over my shoulder. "I feel like I do all the work, and then you guys don't even care!"

"Look, it's true you do all the work," agreed Emma. "But we thought you enjoyed it. If you're tired of it, we can divvy it up, right, girls?" she said, looking at Mia and Katie.

"Sure! Why not?" said Mia, flinging her hair behind her shoulders in the way she does when she's getting down to work.

"Fine," I said.

"I'll do the swim team project, okay?" said Mia.

"And I'll do the Mud Pies," said Emma.

"And I'll do whatever the next big project is," said Katie.

I looked at them all. "What about invoicing, purchasing, and inventory?"

The girls each claimed one of the areas, and even though I was torn about giving up my responsibilities, I was glad to see them shouldering some of the work for a change. We agreed that they would e-mail or call me with questions when they needed my help.

"Great," I said. "Now I'm leaving." And I walked home from Mia's quickly, so fast I was almost jogging. My pace was fueled by anger about the Cupcake Club *and* the desire to get home to my sister, Dylan, as quickly as possible, so I could start asking questions about the pep rally parade and all that it would entail.

CHAPTER 2

The Quest for Cool Begins

*Y*es, it is dorky to go with a friend," said Dylan. "I mean, not totally dorky, like if you go in a group with some guys, too, but just you and another girl? Dor-ky!" she singsonged.

I had made it home from Mia's in record time and rushed up to Dylan's room. She and I get along pretty well, since it's just the two of us sisters and we're both pretty type A, according to my mom. This means we're both hard workers who never stop or compromise until a job is done perfectly. Anyway, it turned out Mia and Katie *were* right about everything. I couldn't decide who I was more annoyed at: them for knowing first about going with a boy to the parade, or Dylan for never mentioning it to me.

I flopped onto her bed, and then I rolled over and groaned. "So who am I going to go with?" I wailed.

Dylan was filing her nails. "Well," she began, pausing to blow at some imaginary piece of dust on her ring finger, "why not Matt?"

Dylan knows I like Matt Taylor because she helped me make myself over to win his attention a little while back. She also knew I wanted to dance with him at her sweet sixteen, which, as I mentioned earlier, I actually did.

"He'll never ask me," I whimpered.

"So? Ask *him*!" said Dylan.

Me? Ask *him* to march with *me* in the parade? Impossible! That was the same as asking him on a date, and there was just no way I'd ever do that!

"Yeah, as if!" I said.

"Why? You're best friends with his sister. You practically live at his house. You've worked on stuff together before. Look, don't forget boys are just as nervous about all this stuff as girls are, and he'd probably be grateful to not have to ask someone."

Ugh. The very idea gave me full-body shivers. "But I'm sure I'm *not* the someone he'd like to go with," I said.

"Why not?" she said, now slicking on clear nail

13

polish with an authoritative swipe. Dylan is nothing if not confident.

"Because I'm not . . . cool," I admitted.

Dylan narrowed her eyes and looked at me. "Well, I can help you with that," she said. "You know I love a challenge."

"Oh no," I said.

"Let me think about it, and I will get back to you with a plan of action tomorrow afternoon, okay?"

"Okay . . . ," I said hesitantly.

But she'd already turned to her computer and begun to type furiously. I guess I am quite the inspiring makeover candidate if she's always willing to take me on.

Double oh no!

That night I sent mini-overview e-mails of the Cupcake Club procedures to Mia, Katie, and Emma, explaining inventory, scheduling, purchasing, and invoicing, along with what we had coming up. I kept feeling like I'd forgotten something, but it was really just that I kept searching for Cupcake Club responsibilities and tasks and finding none. There were no columns of costs to doodle in my journal and no long-range schedules to sketch out. I hadn't realized quite how much time and energy—even my thoughts—the Cupcake Club consumed.

The next day I met up with the rest of the Cupcake Club at the school cafeteria. School hadn't started yet, but Mia had volunteered us to be on the decoration committee for the pep rally, much to my annoyance. (If she was going to volunteer us for something why not the refreshments committee, where we could at least promote our cupcakes?) But I held my tongue. I knew Mia loved anything having to do with design, so this was right up her alley.

On my way to the cafeteria, I met the math department head, Mr. Donnelly, in the hallway. He asked me if I had a few minutes to speak to him. I have an A+ average, so I figured he was just asking me to tutor some kid in the coming school year. Now that I had all this free time, I could say yes. But that wasn't it at all!

"Alexis, I have a great opportunity for you," he said. "I think you should join the Future Business Leaders of America, and I'd be happy to nominate you." He smiled at me happily.

Wow! That was not what I'd been expecting at all! "Oh, Mr. Donnelly! That's . . . that's just sooo great! Thank you! I can't believe I'd be eligible."

My stomach flipped over in excitement, and I got goose bumps up and down my arms.

The Future Business Leaders of America is part of a national organization, and we have a small chapter here at Park Street Middle School. The kids who are in it are by far the smartest kids in the school—the ones who are straight A+ students, honor roll all the way (well, like me, I guess). It's hard to get nominated. You can't ask anyone to nominate you—you have to be chosen, and it's a huge honor. They only choose four kids a year from each grade. And the best part is, the kids meet all the time with the faculty supervisor, who teaches them cool business stuff, like marketing and accounting theories, and then at the end of the year they go to a big convention in the city and meet with all kinds of famous businesspeople. It's supposed to be amazing!

Mr. Donnelly could tell I was thrilled. "I've heard so much about your wonderful Cupcake Club, and of course I sampled the goods at the school fund-raiser last year, and I think you've got a terrific business going. Your hands-on experience running it would bring a lot to the group."

"Well, my friends and I all run it together," I said modestly. But that really wasn't true. Except now, maybe it was. I kind of felt unsure of my

16

role and didn't know what to say. I wondered if I'd be joining the FBLA under false pretenses if Mr. Donnelly thought I ran the whole Cupcake Club by myself.

"You'd be an asset either way. What do you think?"

I mentally scanned my other commitments and my time schedule. "Can I think about it for a day and discuss it with my parents? I have so much on my plate right now," I said. I was so flattered, I wanted to say yes immediately, but it's never good to agree to new responsibilities in a spontaneous fashion.

Mr. Donnelly smiled at me. "Spoken like a true professional," he said. "And absolutely. Let me know. The deadline is in about two weeks, so you have a little time to think about it, but it does look better if you submit early." He winked. "The early bird catches the worm."

"I know it!" I agreed. "Thanks, Mr. Donnelly!"

"Anytime. Just keep me posted!" he said as I sailed off to the cafeteria.

I could hardly wait to tell the others, but when I spotted them across the lunchroom, all sitting together and chatting excitedly, I knew they were not discussing Cupcake business but instead the pep rally parade and what they'd wear and who they'd walk with and all that. I felt myself deflate a little. I couldn't tell them about the FBLA. They wouldn't get it. And, anyway, there was something a tiny bit underhanded about only me getting nominated. After all, it's supposed to be all four of us in business together.

I trudged over to sit with them, dreading the discussion and wishing I could share my real news. It would just have to wait until I got home. My parents and Dylan would be ecstatic for me, I realized. Just picturing their reactions cheered me up a little and gave me the patience to listen to the pep rally chatter.

Dylan wasn't ready for my undorking when I got home, so I went to my room to start reading one more book before summer was over. I had decided to save my news for dinner.

At exactly seven o'clock, I skipped down the stairs to the kitchen table. My parents had come up to say hi when they'd gotten home from work a little earlier, but I'd restrained myself, even though I felt like I was going to burst. I wanted to see everyone's faces at the same time when I told them.

I sat down and waited until everyone had settled and we'd passed around the platter of stir-fried shrimp and veggies, and then I said, "Mom, Dad, Dylly, I have major news. Major *good* news!"

I looked with pleasure at the expectant faces of my family: Mom, Dad, and Dylan.

"Matt asked you to be his parade partner?" said Dylan excitedly.

My parents looked back at me with big smiles on their faces. I was irritated.

"No. Nothing to do with that." Now I wasn't sure how to make the transition. "It's about school," I said.

"Oh! I know! You're going to run for class president!" my dad said, grinning.

This was getting more and more irritating. "No. I am not running for class president," I said through gritted teeth. "This is not a guessing game. I am going to tell you."

"Oh! Sorry, dear," said my mother, blotting her mouth with a napkin. "Because I was going to guess that they put you on varsity tennis."

"Noooo! No more guesses!" I huffed. "Now my news isn't so great. I think I'm going to just keep it to myself," I said. Jeez, the nerve of these people.

"No, we're sorry, sweetheart. What is it? We'll

be thrilled for you no matter what, because if you're happy, we're happy!" said my mom, beaming.

I rolled my eyes.

My mom scolded me. "No pouting, now," she said. "Turn that frown upside down!"

Ugh. I hate when she uses her parenting-class voice on me. It's so humiliating.

"Fine. Mr. Donnelly asked me to join the Future Business Leaders of America. It's a really big deal. Only four kids from each grade are picked—"

"Oh, that's wonderful!" said my mom. "What an honor!"

But Dylan did not have the reaction I was expecting.

"No," she said. "Absolutely not." She folded her arms and leaned on the table, in direct defiance of my mom's strict mealtime-manners code, and she looked me in the eye. "You. Will. Not. Do. It. Do I make myself clear?"

"Wait, what?" I asked. I was confused.

"You have to say no. It's one thing to feel like a dork. It's another to take out a billboard announcing it. The FBLA is for *total* dorks. Complete, unredeemable, dorkorama! You cannot do it. Period." Dylan sat back in her chair and patted her mouth with a napkin. Having said her piece, she was confident I would obey.

"Dylan! That was absolutely inappropriate!" said my mom, in shock.

"Don't listen to your sister, sweetheart. Maybe she's just feeling a little . . . tiny, tiny bit envious," said my dad.

"Ha!" Dylan guffawed. If she'd been drinking her milk at the time, it would have come out of her nose. "That is one thing I am *not*."

I was stunned. Dylan was an overachiever, just like me. How could she not think this was a big, exciting deal?

"Dylan, you need to apologize to your sister. I'm counting to three. One, two . . ."

"Mom!" protested Dylan. "Stop! Alexis has hired me to help her undork herself in time to get a date for the pep rally. She has empowered me to advise her. And this is my first piece of advice: The FBLA is sudden social death. Do not join. If you take even one piece of advice from me, let it be that. I shall say no more on the topic." And she picked up her fork and began eating again.

I, on the other hand, had lost my appetite.

CHAPTER 3

The Commandments of Cool

$\mathcal{M}$y parents banned the topics of dorkiness and the FBLA for the rest of dinner, but it didn't leave us much to talk about since that was all that was on my mind, anyway.

Afterward, I retreated to my room to continue reading my book while they cleaned the kitchen, and then I took a shower. A few moments after I closed my door, someone knocked.

"Come in," I said warily.

Dylan came in holding a file folder and sat on my bed, all serious. "Listen, you're the one who always says 'knowledge is power,'" she began.

I nodded and then shrugged.

"And you *asked* me to give you help and to share my wisdom."

Annoying but true. I nodded again.

"I've put together a report on the state of dorki-ness and how to convert it to coolness in six easy steps. It's all in here." She fanned the folder at me.

I rolled my eyes. I didn't want to play into her hands, but I really did have an urge to grab the folder and devour its contents. Instead, I waited.

"It's up to you which path you take, but I have illuminated the way to coolness for you, and I hope you will make the right choice. And just to reit-erate, the FBLA is *not* the right choice. Nothing personal."

Dylan moved to hand me the folder and I let it hang in the air for an extra second, then I took it from her and tossed it on my desk supercasually, like I didn't really care what it said.

"Thanks," I said finally, good manners winning out over my annoyance with her and her directives.

"Good luck" was all she said as she closed the door behind her.

I stared at the folder, knowing that once I opened it, my life would be forever changed, whether I acted on her advice or not. Maybe I didn't care if I was a dork. Maybe being cool would take up too much time and keep me from doing the things I really wanted to do, like joining the FBLA.

But knowledge is power; it's true that I always say that. And nothing tempts me like a well-done research project sitting inside a folder.

I sighed and picked it up, and then I began to read.

The report was long and involved. Dylan had really done her homework, as usual. There was a long list of "Don'ts" in the Dork section, as well as a list of individuals we both knew who were cited for their dorkiness (including my parents!). There was a filmography part, referencing movies I should see that would help to illuminate the differences between dorks and cool people, and there was a recommended reading list of magazines and blogs that would "cool me up," according to Dylan. It all looked like a lot of work.

But the main body of the report came down to the Six Commandments of Cool, as Dylan called them. They were:

(1) Do well in school, but never mention it. Even deny it at times. (See Section A for examples of when and how to deny.)

(2) Smile and be friendly, but not too friendly. (Do *not* encourage dorks by acting like they are your equals.)

(3)   In public, pretend that you do not care about the following: what you wear, how you look, who likes you. (But in private, DO pay close attention to these things.)

(4)   Do not be too accessible, either via e-mail, online social sites, IM, phone, etc. (and often say you have plans, even if you do not).

(5)   Go with the flow and just let things roll. (It's dorky to make a fuss.)

(6)   Always have a good guy friend. (See Section B for reasons why.)

I slumped in my desk chair and thought about all the advice.

This would be a lot of work. And some of it went against my better instincts. Like, why would I deny getting good grades? That was preposterous to me. And how could I not be friendly to people who were dorks? According to Dylan's list of dorks, many of them were my friends! Maybe not people I'd invite to sleep over, but certainly people I'd pick first as a lab partner in science class. I was suddenly supposed to not be too friendly to them? That would be impossible. And worse, I'd get stuck with a dumb lab partner and get a bad grade!

But the Cool Commandment that was the

25

hardest for me was number six. I really didn't have any guy friends, and I wasn't even sure who'd be a good candidate.

Section B said guy friends were good for stand-ins when you need a date but don't have one (Hellooo, pep rally parade!), and they can introduce you to other guys, one of whom might be boyfriend material. Guy friends also signal to other guys that a girl is okay. Like, if a girl is cool enough to be friends with this guy, then go ahead and like her because she's preapproved or something. Guy friends also give you a good perspective on what boys like in a girl and what's important to them. Also, talking with boys who you are not romantically interested in gives you practice for talking to the ones you *do* like. And so on and so on.

Section B wiped me out. I closed the folder, set it back on my desk, and then just sat there, stunned. I had an urge to do the only thing that would make me feel better: work on the Cupcake Club. But having resigned my duties, there was nothing for me to do.

There was another knock on the door, and this time it was my dad.

"Hi, sweetheart," he said from my doorway. "Can I come in?"

"Hi, Dad," I said. I was happy to see him, but I knew the lecture that was coming. I could have recited it myself.

He came in and sat on the corner of my bed so recently vacated by Dylan. "Alexis, your mom and I and all your friends and all your teachers think you are wonderful just as you are. You are talented, smart, ambitious, organized—"

I interrupted. "Thanks, Dad. But I'm okay. I don't need a pep talk. I really did ask Dylan for her help."

My dad pressed his lips together into a thin line and looked up at the ceiling while he gathered his thoughts. "I guess what your mom and I want you to know is . . . cool is temporary. It's a barometer kids use for a few years, when they are too unsure of themselves to be individuals. So they create this system that evaluates people based on criteria that literally have no bearing on the rest of your life. Trust me, once you are out of middle school and high school, there's no such thing as who's cool and who's not. So we suggest you forget about all that temporary stuff and just follow your passions. Those are what make a person great and attractive to others—being energized and excited about life! Not being boxed in by some rules or regulations . . ."

Boy, would his eyes pop out at Section A, I thought. I tried not to smile. It was just that his advice was such a contrast to Dylan's. I knew he was right when I really thought about it, but the truth was, I *did* have to get through these next few years worrying about the cool factor. That was just a fact of life. Following your passions, if they were dorky, did not exactly get you a partner for the pep rally parade.

"I know, Dad. You guys tell me this all the time," I said, trying to be kind but also wanting him to stop.

"We do?" My dad's face brightened. "Oh good! Then you're actually listening! That's great news!"

I smiled.

"Listen, honey, I just came up here to tell you that your mom and I think you should go for it with the Future Business Leaders of America. And don't listen to anything Dylan the Drama Queen tells you. Even if you did ask for her help. Okay?"

I nodded. "Thanks," I said, though I had every intention of doing the opposite of what he'd just told me.

He stood up and then planted a kiss on my head. "Get some sleep, now. It's late." And he walked out the door.

"Good night, Dad," I said.

I heard my dad enter Dylan's room and start lecturing her. I smiled with happiness, pushing aside the twinge of guilt I felt for bringing this all on Dylan. She really was just trying to help me, after all.

I picked up a pen and chewed on the cap, which is what I always do when I'm thinking. I was at a loss. I kept feeling anxious, like there was something I had to do. Then I'd realize it was the Cupcake Club and that, in fact, there *wasn't* anything for me to do now. I was so stressed about the other girls getting it all done, but at the same time I refused to chase them down with IMs and e-mails to make sure they were. It was just that one or two botched jobs could ruin our business for months, if not for good. When you run a business on word of mouth and good recommendations, your reputation is all you have. I chewed the pen harder.

Finally, I snapped. I decided to send an e-mail to the club to ask them for a Cupcake meeting at lunch tomorrow after our decorations committee discussion. With so many loose ends assigned to other people, we needed a meeting to catch up and to see how things were going, just for the good of the business. I vowed to myself that I would not take over or do any of the other girls' assignments. I just needed to put my mind at ease that the others were doing their jobs.

I hopped onto my e-mail account and sent the group the lunch meeting request. There was an e-mail in my in-box requesting that we do cupcakes for a book club meeting of a friend of Katie's mom. I forwarded it to Katie, since she was doing the scheduling now.

After pressing send, I packed my ledger and CC notebook in my backpack and then went to brush my teeth, wash my face, and get into my pj's. With my retainer in, I called downstairs to my mom that I was ready for her to come up to say good night.

While I waited I climbed into bed and grabbed the Cool folder from my desk. I just couldn't help myself. I flipped it open and then began to read it again.

CHAPTER 4

Go with the Flow

There were lots of kids at school the next day for various pep rally committees: the refreshments committee, the entertainment committee, and, of course, the decorations committee. I strained to hear if anyone was talking about who they'd march with, but I didn't hear any of the other girls mention boys' names. I hated to ask them directly; it would be rude. But I was dying to know if they were marching with boys.

I ran into Mr. Donnelly on the way to the cafeteria, and he immediately wanted to chat about the FBLA.

"Alexis! I haven't heard back from you about the Future Business Leaders of America! Are you interested? Did you discuss it with your parents?" He smiled expectantly at me.

I was a little taken aback. He had just asked me about it the day before! "Um. Oh, Mr. Donnelly. I'm so sorry to be slow on this. It's . . . uh . . . a big decision, and I just need a little more time to assess my workload. I'm sorry. I've just been so swamped with the Cupcake Club," I lied, crossing my toes inside my shoes and feeling guilty. I knew that if it were up to Dylan, I'd say that my parents and I had discussed it and I wasn't going to be able to fit it in for this year and thank you so much. But I still really wanted to do it. The battle raged inside my heart as I struggled not to let on one way or the other.

"Wonderful! Lots of big jobs coming up? All organized?" he asked enthusiastically.

"Uh-huh. You bet!" I said with false confidence. Little did he know, I had absolutely no idea whether things were under control or not, but I couldn't exactly explain that! I'm sure being cool and going with the flow are not quite part of the FBLA agenda.

"All righty then. Just let me know soon, because I don't want to wait until the last minute to propose you. And if you can't do it, I need a little time to find someone else, okay?" he said.

"Absolutely. I'm so sorry for the delay," I agreed. We said good-bye, and I practically ran away.

Being all cool and relaxed sure is stressful.

I met the Cupcakers at our usual table at lunch, my ledger and notebook secured in my bag. I wouldn't take them out unless I absolutely had to. I just couldn't imagine having a meeting without them, but we'd see.

Naturally, the conversation was about the parade as soon as we sat down.

"Mia! I think someone likes you!" said Katie mischievously as I put my tray onto the table.

Mia's face turned pink. "Who?" she asked.

Katie grinned. "Chris Howard! I saw him staring at you on the bus this morning, with his head propped on his hand, all dreamylike!"

Mia's face grew even redder. "Stop! No way, you're just imagining things!" she protested, but she had a little smile, like she was pleased by the idea.

"He'd be great to go with!" said Emma; a little wistfully, I thought. "He's cute and nice, and he's pretty tall!"

Mia nodded, but she seemed like she didn't want to commit.

Katie shrugged. "Anyway, I'm just saying . . ."

"We've still got some time to figure it all out," said Emma.

Mia nodded, happy, it seemed, to change the subject. "Yes. We should at the very least be working on our costumes. There's not that much time. I should organize a schedule, maybe."

"Yes! Please do!" said Katie.

Emma nodded vigorously. "That would be so helpful!" she agreed.

Have these people lost their minds? I wondered.

"Ahem," I said. "A schedule? For costume making?" I looked at each of them, but they didn't understand what I meant. "Hello? How about a schedule for cupcake baking?"

"Oh, Alexis! We're getting to that!" said Katie breezily. "Just let us have our fun first, before you start being a slave driver."

"I thought the *Cupcake Club* was supposed to be fun!" I said. I couldn't help myself.

Emma looked at me, all sympathetic. "It is fun, Alexis. Just . . . not as fun as pep rallies and parades! Come on. Be reasonable. You know that," she said.

"Hmph!" I said. I decided to just eat my lunch while they chattered on, talking about anything but our slowly shriveling business. My mind drifted back to Dylan's directives. *Go with the flow,* I told myself. *Stay cool.*

Fine.

After nearly an hour of costume and decorations chatter, the others finally decided to address the Cupcake Club agenda. I felt like I was about to burst from going with the flow!

"Sorry, Alexis." At least Emma had the decency to remember. "I know you wanted this to also be a Cupcake meeting," she said.

I shrugged, flowing (outwardly at least!).

"So when's the Mud Pie sample baking?" asked Emma.

"Let's do it this Friday at my house," offered Mia. I knew she was trying to make up for her previous lack of interest in the topic, but I wasn't going to be fooled.

"Okay. Have you finalized the order amount for the swim meet?" I asked her. I couldn't help myself. It had been keeping me up at night, worrying about it.

"No, not yet," said Mia casually. "But I will."

"When?" I asked.

Mia narrowed her eyes at me. "Later today. Is that okay, boss?"

I shrugged. "Whatever you want," I said.

"I'm just here to advise, not to boss." As much as I wanted to just let go and be cool, I couldn't. Instead I asked, "Do you know how much they'll be charging for the cupcakes at the fund-raiser?" That was the other thing that had been keeping me up at night.

"Why does that matter to us?" asked Mia, confused.

"Because that is a factor in where we set our wholesale price," I said. How could people not know something so obvious?

"Why?" asked Mia.

I sighed. *Stay cool, just stay cool,* I told myself. "Because if they are only going to charge a dollar and fifty cents for their cupcakes, we can't charge them a dollar and twenty-five cents wholesale. Then the margin is too small for them."

"What's a margin?" asked Katie.

"It's the difference between the buying and selling prices. The profit." I gritted my teeth, but I really wanted to scream. *Really, people? After all this time, you don't even know what a* margin *is?*

"Well, I don't know. But I do have a really cool idea for how to decorate them!" said Mia.

I sighed again. "How's the invoicing coming along?" I asked, turning to Emma. I didn't like to hear myself being such a taskmaster, but with all these loose ends that were driving me crazy, I had to carpe diem! (Seize the day! It's another one of my mottoes.)

Emma sat up straight in her chair. "Oh. Well, I started last night but . . . I felt really tired and went to sleep instead. I'll finish it tonight." She looked uncomfortable.

I was dying to ask if she'd even read my e-mail describing how to do it, but I restrained myself, thinking of Dylan's advice again.

Katie piped up. "I did do the ingredient inventory, though! We need to stock up on everything: eggs, flour, sugar—you name it. And I got your e-mail about the book club event. We're all set for that," she said, obviously proud of herself for being the only one who had actually done some work.

This made me relish bursting her bubble, cool or not.

"But, Katie, we have the swim meet to bake for that day, remember? And for inventory, I'm the one who has all the new stuff from BJ's. I have the new twenty-pound bags of flour and of sugar from last week. Remember? I said it in my e-mail."

Katie seemed to sink in her chair. "Oh."

I had to wonder if they ever read any of the

e-mail updates I sent out. It was starting to seem like they'd gotten in the habit of just ignoring them, knowing I'd take care of everything.

I didn't want my friends to hate me, but I was so incredibly frustrated. I knew it wasn't cool to care so much, but I couldn't help it. The three of them sat there, looking dejected and kind of lost.

"Well . . . anyone else heading home now?" I asked. But no one spoke up. "Then bye! See you later."

I was sure they'd be talking about me behind my back once I left, and I didn't feel so cool with that. Up ahead I spied Janelle Bernstein, my admittedly nerdy friend from science last year, who was also walking in the same direction. I was about to call out to her to wait up, but suddenly Dylan's words echoed in my mind. *Be friendly but not too friendly,* she had said. So I didn't call out. I walked out of the school alone, about twenty-five paces behind Janelle, and very, very lonely.

I decided I didn't want to walk home like I normally do, so I took the bus. Unfortunately, the dreaded girls of the PGC, the Popular Girls Club, decided that they were taking the bus that afternoon too. These girls are cool, and they sure didn't need a research report to tell them how to be that way. They're also mean. Or at least their leader, Sydney Whitman, is. The rest of them are just followers, I guess. Not too bad if you meet up with them somewhere random, one on one, but they're very intimidating in a group.

Anyway, they were, of course, discussing the parade, and everyone else on the bus was all ears. The PGC girls knew they were, and it seemed like they were kind of onstage, hamming it up for the less cool girls who were hanging on their every word.

"I'm going to get fitted for my fairy costume this week!" announced Sydney, as if it was the most solemn and important news of the year. "My mom is taking me into the city to a costume designer she knows, who works on all the big Broadway shows. They're going to hand make the costume—masses of shimmery green tulle and floaty layers. It's going to be breathtaking!"

The PGC girls sighed with envy, all starry-eyed. It was annoying. *Go with the flow, go with the flow,* I reminded myself. Was I uncool for thinking Sydney was taking this all waaay too seriously? If I were cool, would I be more organized and psyched for it myself?

"Have you asked you know who?" Callie

Wilson asked Sydney. My ears perked up. I might learn something since the boy aspect was, of course, the most interesting and stressful part of the parade for me.

You could have heard a pin drop on the bus as everyone awaited Sydney's answer. And we didn't even know who "you know who" was! I was tempted to ask the boy behind me for the time, just to show I didn't care. Except that I did care. So I stayed quiet.

I glanced up to see Sydney grinning, faking modesty. "You'll never believe it, but *he* asked *me*!"

I looked away quickly.

As if Sydney would ever have to ask a boy out, not with her long, white-blond hair and fashion-forward clothes and chic little posse of friends. Not to mention her steamroller attitude. If the boy she wanted hadn't asked her, then I'm sure she would have engineered a way to march with him in the parade. Even if it meant poisoning his date.

I was dying to know who it was.

"How about you? Did lover boy call yet?" Sydney asked Callie.

Oh no! I felt a surge of adrenaline. Sydney must mean Matt Taylor!

Callie also has a crush on Matt Taylor, and she and Sydney have engineered lots of "coincidental" (not!) meetings between the two of them, sometimes when I'm actually there. I think it's mostly Sydney, really. It's like she's Callie's agent, the way she pushes Callie at Matt. Emma doesn't think Matt likes Callie, but it's not like it's exactly bad news if you're a guy and one of the coolest and prettiest girls in the school is after you.

"No," Callie said, all quiet.

WHEW! I wanted to yell. But I didn't (staying very cool!), and I had no excuse to stick around since the bus had arrived at my stop. I stood up to get off.

Sydney had a shocked look on her face. "Then _you'll_ just have to ask _him!_" she said to Callie.

"Me? Call Matt? And ask him myself?"

Aha! So it was Matt. The idea sickened me. I started to walk down the bus aisle to leave.

I was happy to see that Callie clearly didn't like Sydney's idea.

"If you don't, I will. And that will look worse!" said Sydney.

I glanced at Callie one last time as I left the bus. She looked stricken, like Sydney had slapped her. Which I guess she kind of had.

Sydney is really just a bully who likes to push people around, I thought for the millionth time. Well, she wasn't going to push me around too. I needed to do something to get Matt to agree to be my date. But what?

CHAPTER 5

Half Cool

Friday afternoon, after finishing up some more pep rally decorations at school, we went to Mia's house for a baking session. I was feeling really disconnected from the other girls because I hadn't been sending them Cupcake e-mails and, I noticed, none of them had been e-mailing me about anything. I was starting to wonder if we'd still be friends if we didn't have the Cupcake Club. I also wondered if we'd still have the Cupcake Club if I wasn't running it. These were both nerve-wracking thoughts.

As we walked to Mia's, Callie caught up with us on the sidewalk and walked a few blocks with us. I noticed her looking over her shoulder, as if to make sure Sydney didn't see her. Sometimes Callie is friends with us because she and Katie were best friends growing up, and their moms are still best friends. It's hard for them. It's like they're friends when they're alone together but not in public.

I tried to act cool, which meant basically not talking. I hoped some other kids like Janelle would see me walking with Callie and assume I was cool, maybe even in the PGC too. I looked around, but no one seemed to notice or care.

Anyway, as we walked, the others were discussing our eighth grade math placement test, which had been really hard. Even Emma, who usually gets really good grades, had thought she bombed it. I, on the other hand, was pretty sure I had aced it. We hadn't gotten our schedules yet, so we didn't know who made it into math honors.

"How do you think you did, Alexis?" asked Callie, trying to gauge how well she did.

I don't like to brag about grades, but I'm usually honest with my friends. Except this was Callie, who was not my friend. "Oh, I . . ." I was about to say I was sure I'd be scheduled for Mr. Donnelly's math honors class when I remembered Dylan's advice: Get good grades, but never mention it. So I clammed up. "I did okay," I said, and shrugged. It felt so weird to give the impression that I was less prepared or less smart than I really am. It felt like I was wearing a shirt that was three sizes too small.

Callie nodded, probably assuming I'd be in regular math like the rest of them. If one of the other girls had pressed me, I might have told the truth. But I didn't want Callie to think I was a dork, so I just left it like that.

Naturally, the conversation next turned to Topic Number One: the pep rally and the costume parade.

"Sydney's got us all organized," said Callie. "She says we each have to have a date and a particular kind of costume." She laughed it off, but her eyes weren't smiling along with her mouth. "What are you guys doing?"

Katie and Mia took the lead, discussing their costume plans and Katie's potential date with either Joe or George. Katie announced that Chris had asked Mia to go with him, but that she hadn't accepted yet because she was waiting to hear if a guy she liked in the city might come.

I was mortified. This was all news to me! I looked at Emma to see if she'd known any of this stuff, and it was clear that she was totally up-to-date. I was the only one in the dark! I wasn't about to look clueless in front of Callie by asking all sorts of questions, but as we walked on, I started to get really, really mad. After all, I work my butt off to include everyone in the Cupcake Club on every decision and every plan. And now they go making all sorts of plans without me!

Then the worst part came.

"What about you two?" Callie asked me and Emma.

"Oh, um . . ." I had nothing to say. No costume plan, no marching partner who was a boy. Should I have just announced that I'm a hopeless loser and got it over with? Put myself out of my misery?

But then Emma said, "I'm marching with my brother. We're going to be wizards together."

My stomach dropped and my heart lurched. *Really?* I looked quickly at Callie's face to see if it showed any emotion, but she must've been really good at "going with the flow" because she just nodded and looked away, saying, "Cool. Well, I'm heading off here." We all said good-bye to her and kept on walking to Mia's.

Now I was getting madder than I already was. I dropped back behind the others and brooded. Emma had known I was dying to go with Matt, and now she'd asked him and planned a matching costume with him. Talk about an opportunist!

Maybe I just wouldn't go after all!

I walked in silence while Mia and Katie chattered away. After about half a block, Emma dropped back and fell into step beside me. Then she turned to me and said, "You know I was just saying that so she wouldn't ask him, right?"

"What?" I was still blazing with anger, so I couldn't quite process what Emma had said.

"I'm not marching with Matt. I just didn't want Callie to!" said Emma.

The truth dawned on me, and I could feel my whole mood turn around, all my gripes forgotten. "What? *Really?*" I yelled, totally elated now. "Emma, you're the best!" I grabbed her in a big hug, even though I'm not much of a hugger, and Katie and Mia turned to look at us in confusion as I swung Emma around like a rag doll.

"Stop! Enough! Put me down!" yelled Emma, and finally, I did.

"What's all this about?" asked Mia.

"Emma is not marching with Matt."

"But you'd better ask him before someone else tries to," said Emma, wagging her finger at me.

"Do you think Callie would do that? Even though she knows you're marching with him? Or thinks you are?" I asked.

47

Emma shrugged. "Maybe not. But Sydney would."

"Hmm. Good point," I said. I guess I wasn't out of the woods yet. Plus, Emma had said I'd need to ask him.

Gulp. I had to figure this out fast!

Mia hadn't requested any ingredients from me, and I hadn't brought any, so we had to kind of scrounge around her house for our ingredients. Luckily, her mom had bought supplies for some cookies she was baking for her clients, so there was enough flour and sugar and butter to go around.

I was irritated, though. I almost wished Mia hadn't had the supplies, just so everyone could see the importance of planning ahead and being organized. Instead, Mia managed to slide by without doing any of the usual prep work that I had to coordinate for our baking sessions.

We had three batches going: one of Mud Pie samples, one of swim meet samples, and one for the book club Katie had double booked for us.

We usually have to bake mini cupcakes for Mona's bridal shop every Friday, but thank goodness Mona was on vacation and her shop was closed. I don't think we could have handled another order.

While we baked, we played one of our favorite games. It was easier than having a real conversation. Less stressful.

"Okay . . . orange cream cheese frosting, cinnamon pumpkin cake, a few candy corns on top, and orange wrappers . . . ," said Mia.

"Jack-o'-lanterns, of course!" said Katie. "That's too easy."

"Or you could call them Halloweenies!" said Emma with a laugh.

I wanted to be lighthearted and go with the flow, but I was stressing about the other girls' lack of plans for our upcoming events. I searched for a conversational opening in order to bring it up. Finally, when Katie had stumped the others with a request to name "marble cake, marble frosting, marbleized cupcake wrappers," I jumped in.

"Hey, um, I'm just wondering, speaking of marbles . . . Um, maybe I'm losing mine . . . but, Mia, what did you say the plan is for the swim meet cupcakes?"

Mia was making the Mud Pie frosting with cocoa powder, sugar, and butter. It was hard work to mix it, and she was almost panting with the effort. "Well . . . ," she huffed. "I was thinking we'd do white cake, with silver wrappers, and"—*huff*,

49

puff—"swimming-pool blue frosting!" She paused to blow a lock of hair upward and out of her face. "And we'll lay them all out in the shape of a wave!" She smiled triumphantly at us.

"Cute!" said Emma.

I nodded. But Mia hadn't understood my question. I had to ask again.

"So, like, what are we charging them wholesale and how many cupcakes do we need and what's our unit cost? What's our timetable that day, now that we also have a book club to bake for?" I pressed, studiously avoiding looking at Katie, who was responsible for the double booking.

Mia stared up at the ceiling, like she was thinking. "Oh, I don't know. I'll confirm the cupcake count with them. For the wholesale price we can just kind of wing it, right?"

"Wing it?" I said. I felt like she wasn't speaking English. I just wasn't comprehending. I shook my head, as if I was clearing it.

"You know what I mean!" protested Mia. "They tell us the quantity and their retail price and then we can just back it out from there."

I shrugged. "I guess. That's not how we usually do it."

"But it will work, right?" said Mia.

Flow. Go with it. "Sure."

By the end of our baking session, we had reached a temporary truce, and I was feeling a little more included and up-to-date on everyone. We discussed Chris Howard. (Apparently Mia likes him but had been holding out to see if she could get a boy from her old school to come out for the pep rally. In the end she gave up because the travel logistics were too much.) So Mia said yes to Chris, and we joked that they could go as Angelina Jolie and Brad Pitt. We laughed really hard just thinking about it.

Katie told us she had decided to go with George because he had asked her first, and he was willing to dress up as an astronaut while she was a genie. They were just going as friends, even though "he'd like it to be more," according to Katie. We all whooped and hollered at that.

Emma and I looked at each other. "We'd better get cracking on this," she said quietly.

"I know. I guess I need Dylan's help," I said.

Emma knows Dylan almost as well as I do. "Oh no, it's come to that?" she joked.

"Unfortunately, yes," I said, and we laughed.

The first thing I did when I got home was attack Dylan and beg her to go to the Chamber Street

Mall with me the next day to work on my costume. I was surprised, but she readily agreed. It did make me wonder why she was so willing to help me. Was it because it looked bad for her to have a sister who was a dork? Was it because it was a fun hobby for her, making people over? Worst of all, was I such a dork that she felt sorry for me?

In any case, I was glad to have her help. I only hoped she wouldn't tire of the project and give up, leaving me only half cool. That was always a possibility.

Anyway, I decided to not ask too many questions but instead to just . . . you guessed it! Go with the flow!

But that night in bed, I tossed and turned, thinking about the pep rally parade and Matt, my costume, and the Cupcake Club jobs. At about one a.m., I decided that above all, I had to take charge of one thing: the costume. That way, even if I ended up marching with my grandma, at least I'd look good. Right?

CHAPTER 6

I Survived Shopping at Icon

$\mathscr{T}$he Chamber Street Mall is pretty big and pretty good. You have to have an idea of what you want before you go or you can waste lots of time going upstairs and down, back and forth.

Dylan had brainstormed a list of costume ideas, printed out a map of the mall at home, and made a plan of attack for all the shops we'd need to hit. My mom offered to take us, though I wasn't exactly psyched about that. First of all, it's not very cool to shop with your mom; even *I* know that. And second of all, whenever she and Dylan shop together, it turns into a war zone. They always fight about price, what's appropriate, how long it's taking to make a decision, and so on. The bottom line is: My mom hates to shop and Dylan loves it.

In the car, I looked over the list.

"Dylan, some of this is just . . . I mean, are you kidding me? Marilyn Monroe?"

"Oh, Dylly! No!" said my mom in alarm.

Dylan fumed. "Look, I was just brainstorming and trying to think of things that were kind of pretty and not too dorky."

"I'm all for dorky!" my mom said.

Dylan rolled her eyes at me from the front seat. (She always gets the front seat; it's not even a question.) "We know, Mom," she said.

"We'd better hear the rest of it," said my mom, skillfully piloting the car into the mall's parking lot.

"So . . . 'Marilyn Monroe, hippie chick, Pippi Longstocking'?" I read out. "Even *I* know that's dorky!"

"Oooh, I love that idea!" cried my mom "Braids and knee socks! With your red hair, it will be adorable!"

"Yuck!" I continued to read as we parked. "'Night sky' . . . What's that?"

"All black—leggings, long-sleeved T-shirt, socks, and shoes, and then silver or glow-in-the-dark star stickers all over," said Dylan.

"Hmm. That's kind of cool," I said. "'Cow girl, Gypsy, angel, cat'—kind of babyish, Dyl—'fairy . . .'

No can do," I said, thinking of Sydney.

"Fairy! That's it! That would be the best one!" said my mom enthusiastically. "Great idea, Dylly!" We all climbed out of the car, and my mom and Dylan collected their purses and my mom locked the car.

"I know," agreed Dylan. "Once I hit on that one, I almost just scrapped the rest of the list. It's pretty, it's current, and it has a lot of possible variations. . . ."

"And it is not happening," I said vehemently. "Sorry to burst your bubble."

They looked at me in shock. They'd been so engrossed in agreeing about this idea that they hadn't realized I wasn't on board.

"Why ever not?" asked my mom.

"Because," I said. It was too hard to explain, and also kind of humiliating.

"Don't write it off so quickly," said my mom. "We can look around at the other ideas, but keep this one in your back pocket. I'm sure we'll come back to it in the end."

Store number one was the costume store, and it was very picked over. There were a handful of interesting costumes left, but they'd obviously been tried on and shoved back into their plastic bags, so they looked kind of dirty and used. Plus, most of those store-bought costumes were kind of junky and uncomfortable. I wanted to make a bigger statement than just a little polyester and some funny glasses. My reputation might be riding on it.

We went to Big Blue, which is my favorite store. Dylan thought maybe we'd find some bell-bottom jeans and flowing tie-dyed shirts for a hippie look, but those styles were over, and everything was preppy.

"Ooh! How about a nerd?" said my mom, lifting up a plaid sweater vest.

Dylan and I looked at each other and then burst out laughing. "I don't need a *costume* for that, Mom!" I said.

"Don't be ridiculous, sweetheart," said my mom. But I knew from Dylan's silence that she agreed with me. She was just being polite because Mom was there.

We looked in the fabric store and in Claire's, just to get a feel for what they had. And finally we were at Icon, which is Dylan's favorite store in the world and my least favorite. The music is too loud, the aroma too strong, and the lighting too dark. It totally overloads my senses. Luckily, my mom feels the same way.

"Dylan, I think I'll just wait outside if you don't mind," said my mom.

Lucky!

"But, Mom!" Dylan pouted. I think she was hoping she'd hook my mom into buying her something, too, if she came in. I felt bad for Dylan, but I could totally relate to my mom.

"Why don't we do a preview scan, and then I'll get Mom to come look at our choices," I said. I always end up being the diplomat with these two.

They agreed, and in Dylan and I went.

Boom, boom went the music, and *blink, blink* went my eyes, and *GAG* went my throat, which was filled with tea-rose perfume and some other smoky scent I did not like.

"Isn't this great?" yelled Dylan. "Come over here where they keep the new stuff!"

Dylan and I turned a corner and almost crashed into Sydney and the rest of the PGC. Ugh.

I grabbed Dylan and tried to steer her down another aisle, but she was having none of it.

"Aren't those girls from your class?" she asked, rooted to the spot, refusing to budge.

I tried to drag her away. "Yes, but they're not my—"

"Hey, Alexis!" Callie called over the music.

"Hey," I said, suddenly feeling like a total dork to be shopping with my sister.

I saw Sydney shoot Callie a glare for saying hi to me, but then do a double take when she saw Dylan.

"Who have we here?" said Dylan, pouring on the charm all of a sudden. "Are you girls from Lexi's class?"

Oh gosh, why did she have to call me by my private family nickname in front of these girls?

Sydney narrowed her eyes and sized up Dylan. I could literally see her ticking things off a mental checklist. Cool outfit? Check. Pretty? Check. Good figure? Check. Only then did she put out her hand to introduce herself.

"Sydney Whitman," she said, tossing her blond hair in kind of a snotty, confident way.

Not to be outdone, Dylan took Sydney's hand and shook it, tossing her own hair. "Dylan Becker. You're the one who crashed my sweet sixteen," she said, regaining the upper hand. I saw Sydney cringe a little. *Yahoo! Score one for Dylan,* I thought. Maybe this wouldn't be all bad.

The other girls drew near, sensing their leader had respect for this new alpha female in their midst. I stuck close to Dylan's side, hoping some of the halo of her coolness would cast its protective light over me too.

Dylan and Sydney began a weird competitive shopping thing, where they'd each pull something out and show it to their little team (me and the PGC, respectively). They'd make comments about how you could accessorize it to make a total look. This was all well and good, but none of it was helping me find a costume.

"So, what are you girls dressing up as for the parade?" asked Dylan.

"Fairies," said Sydney breezily.

Dylan looked at me like *Gotcha!* "That's so funny! So is Lexi!"

But I shook my head emphatically. "No, actually. I'm not."

Sydney was staring at me like she'd just noticed me. She tilted her head to the side. "So what *are* you going as?" she asked. Everyone waited.

"Uhhhh . . . maybe . . . Marilyn Monroe?" I said.

"Cool!" said Callie. But Sydney shot her a look, and she shut up.

"But you have red hair!" said Sydney.

Suddenly there was someone standing beside me, saying, "Haven't you ever heard of a blond wig?" It was Mia!

I'd never been so happy to see someone in all my life, even if she did stink at scheduling and pricing. "Mia!" I cried, and I hugged her. Thank goodness she didn't act surprised by the hug, but instead hugged me back. I looked over her shoulder and saw her mom. "And Mrs. Valdes!" I cried. Another lifeline.

Mrs. Valdes said, "Alexis, *mi amor*," and double kissed my cheeks, European-style.

I turned to introduce Dylan and saw her and all of the PGC staring wide-eyed at Mrs. Valdes, who is gorgeous and probably the most chic person you'll ever meet in real life. She is a fashion stylist and always has on the latest styles, tweaked just so. Today she looked amazing in a riding outfit: black leggings, knee-high brown-and-black boots, and a longish fitted blazer with slanted pockets and a velvet collar. Her hair was in a bun, and she had on big gold knots for earrings.

"What are you up to?" I asked.

"Costumes, of course! I'm here to find a base for my witch dress that my mom can have Hector sew things onto," said Mia. Hector is Mrs. Valdes's kind of sewing wizard. He makes samples and stuff for her.

"Cool!" I said, remembering Mia's sketch from the Cupcake meeting.

"Do you need help too, *mi amor?*" asked Mrs. Valdes. "You know I love to dress gorgeous redheads!" She always makes a big deal about loving my hair, even though I don't see at all why.

Dylan nudged me, looking at Mrs. Valdes

"Oh, duh! Sorry! Mrs. Valdes, this my sister, Dylan." I said.

"Of course, darling. Dylan, Mia just adores you, and I remember seeing photos from your fabulous party," she said, shaking Dylan's hand. "I love your outfit!"

Dylan actually blushed and smiled. "I've heard a lot about you, Mrs. Valdes. Alexis loved being in your wedding!"

I glanced at the PGC and saw they were hanging on their every word.

"Let's go look at the dresses in the back!" said Mia. She linked her arm through mine and pulled me away.

It looked like Mrs. Valdes thought we might introduce her to the PGC, but through unspoken agreement, Mia and I knew we would not.

"Bye!" we said, and we wiggled our fingers at them as we walked away. Dylan was now in an animated conversation with Mia's mom about hemlines and trends.

It wasn't long before Mrs. Valdes and Dylan had pulled a bunch of dresses for me and Mia to try. Mrs. Valdes was enthusiastic about one of them in particular for me. It was long and white and flowy in a fabric called jersey. I don't know if she was thinking Marilyn Monroe too or what she had in mind, but I wasn't about to second-guess a professional. Mia and I squeezed into the tiny, dark dressing room together and tried on the things.

Once I had on the white dress, I stepped outside. It was hard to see because it was so dark. I walked to the end of the hall and stood in front of a mirror under a lone spotlight.

"Oooh! *Yes!*" Mrs. Valdes clapped her hands and strode over to my side. Dylan followed.

Dylan was sizing me up. "It is very flattering," she agreed. "But not exactly Marilyn Monroe. Not at that length. Are you thinking we would shorten it?"

Meanwhile, the PGC had walked up and were waiting on a newly formed line for a fitting room. They too were sizing me up and whispering. I cringed. Then I thought of Commandment Three (since I've memorized them all): *In public, pretend that you do not care about the following: what you wear, how you look, who likes you. (But in private, DO pay close attention to these things.)* I tossed my hair and stood stock-still while Mrs. Valdes and Dylan brainstormed.

"I'm thinking maybe snow princess!" said Dylan.

"Love it!" said Mrs. Valdes She tapped her chin with her finger. "Or . . ." She gathered the fabric at my left and right shoulders and bunched it together, so it looked like thick straps. "Hector can gather and sew these, and we can pin on some vintage brooches and make her a Greek goddess!"

"Yes!" yelled Dylan.

I could tell the PGC was straining to hear what we were saying. I smiled smugly at them, like a real snow princess, or an ice princess for that matter, and let them wonder what we were discussing.

Then Mia came out, and I relinquished my spot and watched her get the Dylan-and–Mrs. Valdes treatment. By now the line had gotten shorter, and the PGC was within earshot.

"Hop back up, honey," Mrs. Valdes said to me, "and let's get another look, so Dylan and I can figure out the accessories." She began listing: strappy tie-up Roman sandals, a garland of greens for my hair, a gold lamé belt . . .

"Won't all that turn Matt's head!" said Dylan enthusiastically.

Wait, what?

"Matt who?" said Sydney while I was still standing there in shock.

Dylan turned to her. "Matt Taylor, of course! Lexi's marching with him in the parade!"

I turned every shade of red at that moment. I sneaked a peek at Callie, and she was red too.

"Wait, *the* Matt Taylor?" said Sydney, mad all of a sudden.

"The one and only!" singsonged Dylan. "You know he and Alexis have always been close."

I was speechless. *Oh gosh, Dylan. What have you done?* I thought. *Play it cool. Go with the flow.* But the flow had turned into a tidal wave!

Sydney turned to Callie and whispered furiously into Callie's ear.

"But I never had a chance!" protested Callie. And Sydney whispered again.

The only part I caught was "a dork like her!" I knew she meant me.

Callie eyed me guiltily.

"Tonight!" commanded Sydney, and Callie jumped.

Then their number was called, and they hustled into their fitting room, all four of them, like sardines in a can. I was left with my bubble totally burst, feeling like the least powerful goddess on Mount Olympus.

CHAPTER 7

Style Versus Substance

The rest of the Icon expedition was a blur. I hurried out of my costume and ran outside to tell Mom we found something. I wanted to go wait in the car, but Dylan said that would be rude to Mrs. Valdes, who was going to help us find the rest of the accessories, and my mom said it was dangerous for kids to stay in parking lots alone.

So I hid behind a planter.

I heard the PGC come out of the store, and I flattened myself, hoping they weren't coming my way. I was furious at Dylan! How could she have blurted out a lie like that about me and Matt? But worst of all was hearing Sydney call me a dork.

I mean, I know it's kind of true. Look, I like

school and don't mind homework. And I really don't care that much about things like school dances and pep rallies. It's just hard to hear it said out loud like that, plain as day. Especially from someone like Sydney. Especially when it's said with anger. I really wanted to cry. I wondered if Dylan heard Sydney say it. If she did, she ignored it.

Thank goodness the PGC went in the other direction, and then my mom and Mia and Dylan and Mrs. Valdes were soon upon me. Dylan and Mrs. Valdes were chattering happily and my mom and Mia were commiserating about Icon and how overwhelming it is.

I wanted to get Mia alone and ask her what I should do. I knew she would know. The truth about Mia is, she actually had a chance to be in the PGC. But she chose us, the Cupcake Club, instead. I always appreciated that about her, but it also gave her a social standing that was a little above the rest of us, which I sometimes liked and sometimes hated. On the plus side, it made her kind of our senior advisor when it came to social stuff. She was just good at it and a little more savvy. It's probably because she grew up in the city before she lived here.

In the shoe store, while Dylan scouted the sale

area for appropriate goddess sandals, Mia pulled me aside.

"Listen, I heard what happened in there. It's not your problem. You weren't the one who said it. No one could hold you to it."

I wondered if she'd heard Sydney call me a dork too. I could feel my eyes welling up with tears, but I didn't want to cry here. It was unprofessional. What if a client saw me? I sniffed and took a deep breath, then I touched my cuff to each eye to blot the tears.

Mia put her hands on my shoulders and looked at me carefully. "There is one radical thing you could do to make this all better," she said.

"What?" I croaked.

"Ask Matt to march with you."

"Oh, for goodness sake!" That wasn't the answer I wanted to hear.

"I'm serious, though. I know he'd say yes. He likes you, Alexis," she said.

No way. I shook my head. "I could never," I said. "What if he said no?"

"Even if he said no, which I doubt he would, I think he's smart enough and nice enough not to just say no, you know? He'd say something like, 'Oh man, I told Joe I'd march with him and be Tweedledee and Tweedledum' or something. . . ."

I had to laugh at that image and at Mia's imitation of him talking. Mia laughed too. "At the very least he's a good guy. He wouldn't embarrass you," she said. "And no one would have to know."

I thought about it. Would Matt tell Emma? Would he tell Callie? I pictured him saying, *Oh sure, Callie. You'll save me from going with that dork Alexis.*

"Alexis!" Mia said. "Come on! Just think about it. Anyway, you know you'll be looking great!"

With that we rejoined the shopping party and put together the rest of the things Mia and I needed for our costumes.

That night at the dinner table, Dylan could not stop raving about Mrs. Valdes and how cool she was.

"Would you like to trade moms?" asked my mom. "Because I'm going to start getting a complex!"

"But she's so chic! Imagine having someone so stylish living in your very own house! Imagine having access to her closet! I can't believe Mia doesn't just go hog wild every day!" said Dylan.

My mom and I rolled our eyes at each other, and my dad slurped his soup, oblivious.

"Mia is very cool too," said Dylan. "Not quite as cool as Sydney and her gang, but cool. Alexis, why don't you try to hang out more with those girls? They know what cool is."

"I *have* friends. And, anyway, the PGC are not nice. In fact, they're horrible, and they treat people badly. You know that," I said. Then I added, "Plus, I'd be friends with Mia even if she wasn't cool."

"That's your problem right there," said Dylan. "You have no standards. Don't sell yourself short. You and Mia could be friends with those girls. I don't know about Emma and Katie. You'd probably have to ditch them. They're kind of just luggage, but you two should go for it."

I winced. How could she say that about Emma and Katie?

My dad stopped slurping. "Dylan, you've got to be kidding me. Are we talking about Alexis's dearest friends as if they were slabs of beef?"

Dylan looked indignant. "I'm just trying to help," she said.

"You're not helping," said my dad. "Case closed."

"Whatever," said Dylan. And she finished her dinner in silence.

That night I heard my dad trudge up the stairs and give Dylan his old style-versus-substance lecture. We'd all heard it a few times, and it was about how to value the important things in life and how not to follow trends or overvalue superficial things. When he said it, it always made sense, but as soon as he walked away, you could feel yourself weakening and slipping back into bad habits almost immediately.

In my room, I sat there stressing, wondering whether Callie had called Matt yet to ask him out. Or if, in fact, she would. I couldn't stop thinking about it. Only one thing would distract me from all this, and I wasn't supposed to do it. But my fingers itched to get on the keyboard and organize. Finally, I couldn't resist doing a little research for the swim meet job. After all, Mia and her mom had been so nice and helpful to me today, the least I could do was repay the favor, right?

First, I went online to see if I could get a sense of how many people showed up for these regional swim meets. After some searching and doodling of numbers, I figured out an average of about one hundred and twenty attendees. That would mean about ten dozen cupcakes. We'd have to get up really early next Saturday to get that going, and we'd probably have to bake at Emma's because they have two ovens. I'd have to bring over the flour, sugar, eggs, and butter when I went, but it was worth it because baking at Emma's could mean a Matt sighting! My stomach clenched at the idea of him. Was Callie calling him right now? Would he find out what Dylan had told the PGC about us marching together? I decided I'd better warn Emma, in case it did get back to him, so she could defend my honor. I picked up the phone and dialed the Taylors', absentmindedly clicking through the regional swim meet photos on my computer.

Suddenly something occurred to me as I looked at all those photos of people in their bathing suits and the steamy windows in the big indoor pool rooms. It was going to be hot in there! And one thing that doesn't do well in the heat is buttercream frosting!

"Darn it!" I said out loud, just as someone picked up at the Taylors'.

"Uh, hello?"

It was Matt!

Oh no . . . I wanted to hang up! But caller ID! He would know it was me! What should I do?

"Hello? Alexis?"

Oh NO! He *did* know it was me!

"Uh, oh, hi. Matt?"

"Yup. What were you saying when I picked up?" he asked, sounding confused.

"Oh, nothing. Just . . . I just realized something bad on my computer right then, so . . ."

This was so awkward. My adrenaline surged. Should I just ask him? Right now? Should I do it? YES.

"Um, anyway, I was wondering—"

"Hello? Alexis?" It was Emma. She'd picked up on another phone!

"Oh, hey! Hi! There you are!" I said with relief. I felt like I was climbing down from the high dive, legs all shaky.

"Well, bye," said Matt.

"Oh, okay. Bye, Matt," I said.

"What's up?" asked Emma.

And then I started to laugh like a maniac, and I couldn't stop. It was giddy laughter, which was better than crying. I realized I couldn't tell Emma the story now—not over the phone. Not when there was a chance Matt might pick up and hear his name and stay on to listen. That's what I'd do, anyway, if it were me, whether or not it's cool.

"Okaaay . . . ," said Emma. "So why did you call, exactly?"

I didn't want to tell her about the cupcakes that would melt at the swim meet, and I didn't want to tell her about being called a dork at the mall,

73

and I didn't want to tell her how much I loved her brother and hated my sister, even though I *did* want to tell her all of that. So I just decided to go with the flow. I said, "No reason. Just called to say hi."

"Okay. Hi," she said. And then we both started laughing really hard. Emma really is my best friend.

Luggage. Hmph!

CHAPTER 8

A Flirting Failure

At our pep rally committee meeting on Monday, Mia and I filled the Cupcake Club in on what had happened at the mall. I apologized profusely to Emma for putting her and/or Matt in an awkward position, but she waved it off.

"Anyway, he'd probably think it was funny, girls fighting over him at Icon. Hard to imagine old Stink Foot generating that kind of adoration," she said with a laugh.

"So did, uh . . . did Callie call him?" I ventured.

"Nope. Not as far as I know. I can scroll through caller ID when I get home and find out for sure."

"Thanks," I gushed. I was relieved, but not totally relieved. I wouldn't be until I knew for sure. Now I had to think about whether I was going to ask him myself. And if so, how and when?

Just then Chris Howard walked by with his friends, and he and Mia waved and smiled at each other.

"I'm so jealous of your love life," said Emma sadly.

"Don't be. It's not love. It's just a little bit of like," said Mia, all cool.

"On your part," said Katie knowledgeably.

"Well, whatever."

"At least you have someone to march with. Alexis and I are going to be stuck marching together," said Emma.

"Well . . ." I actually wasn't planning on marching with Emma if I couldn't find anyone. I had promised myself that if it came to that, I just wouldn't go. Better to be thought a fool than to show up and prove it. That's another one of my mottoes.

"Wait, you *are* going to march with me, right? I mean, if these girls have dates, who else would I go with?" she asked, gesturing at Katie and Mia.

I decided to turn it into a joke. "It depends on your costume," I said.

"I'm being a hippie," said Emma.

I tapped my chin and acted like I was evaluating

her idea. She swatted me and said, "Shut up! You know we're marching together, so just stop!"

Not if I can help it, I thought, but I didn't say it aloud. Cool Commandment Four rolled through my mind: *Do not be too accessible . . . say you have plans, even if you do not.*

It was time to change the subject.

"Hey, so, um, getting back to my favorite topic . . ."

"Matt or the Cupcake Club?" said Mia wryly, and the others laughed.

I tossed my head and then sat up straight. "The club, of course. Jeez. Anyway, I know it's not my project or anything, but it's going to be pretty hot at the swim meet, you know? So I was wondering, is butter cream the best option?"

The others looked at me blankly.

"Because, you know, it will probably melt and then slide off," I added.

"Oh," said Mia. "Well. I already agreed on the recipe and the price with them."

"What price?" I asked. I couldn't help myself. She should have checked with me before she agreed to anything.

"One dollar a unit?" Mia didn't sound confident.

"One dollar a unit? But we never make

cupcakes for that price! It's always at least a dollar and twenty-five cents! We'd be losing money at one dollar a unit! This isn't a volunteer organization! What are they selling them for?" I tried not to lose my cool, but I felt like my head was going to pop off.

"Three dollars each?" said Mia sheepishly.

"So they make two dollars a cupcake and we lose money? That is a nightmare. We should be splitting the profit, which is standard in almost any industry, or at the very least taking twenty-five percent." I put my head in my hands. I knew something like this was going to happen!

I looked up, and the other three Cupcakers were glancing nervously at one another.

"Can you fix it?" Mia asked finally.

"Look. I'll figure something out. Just . . . next time, make sure you check first. Or, sorry—you should be making the decisions on your own, but at least consult the e-mails I sent you with the overview of how everything runs, okay?"

Mia nodded. "Sorry," she said.

"I liked it better when you were in charge, I think," said Emma.

"Yeah, well . . ." I wanted to say, *So did I*. But I didn't. It wouldn't have been cool.

✿

The rest of the week was a blur of doing but not doing Cupcake Club work, avoiding the FBLA decision and Mr. Donnelly, dodging the PGC, reading the articles Dylan clipped for me from magazines (if *Teen Magazine* tells me to "be a free spirit," which I'm totally not, but also to "always be true to yourself," then which is it?), and relentlessly checking in with Emma to make sure Callie hadn't called Matt. It was stressful, to say the least.

By the end of the week, all I wanted was to curl up in my room with a good Cupcake Club worksheet in front of me and relax. But it was not to be.

On Friday afternoon we went to Emma's to bake for the book club job Katie had taken on. We decided we'd wake up early on Saturday to bake for the swim meet. Matt wasn't going to be home, according to Emma, so I felt a little more relaxed when we got there, but also a little less psyched than normal.

The book club order wasn't that big of a job, and they'd requested one of our old standbys, caramel cupcakes with bacon frosting, so it would be easy for us to make. The only problem was that Katie had forgotten to do the preshopping for the ingredients, and there was no bacon at the Taylors'.

"Okay, well . . . I guess a quick bike ride to the Quickie Mart to buy some bacon is in order," I said. I wasn't going to volunteer. It wasn't me who had forgotten.

"I'll go. It's my fault," said Katie. "Could I have some Cupcake Club money, please?"

I looked at Emma. "Our account is empty. But Emma must have received the payments on those invoices she sent, right?"

Emma looked sheepish. "Um. I haven't had a chance to send them yet. Honestly, Alexis! I don't know how you do it! Between flute practice and baking and dog walking . . . there just isn't time!"

I shrugged. "You have to make time," I said.

Everyone sat there looking morose.

Finally, I sighed. I wanted to teach these people a lesson, but I also didn't want to run the Cupcake Club into the ground.

"Fine. Look, I always keep a cushion of cash for the business. It's called capital. You aren't supposed to use it except maybe, maybe in an emergency. I guess this is a small emergency." I reached into my book bag and pulled out a portfolio-style wallet.

Inside I had bank envelopes filled with bills of different denominations.

"Wow, Alexis, how much is in there?" asked Katie.

"We've saved a hundred dollars. I think we probably only need to take out ten right now, for the bacon, unless there's anything else you think we might need. What about tomorrow, Mia?" I asked. I didn't want to be the taskmaster, but this was getting ridiculous.

Mia bit her lip and looked at the ceiling, as if mentally reviewing her list. "Actually, we could use some silver foil cupcake papers," she said.

I sighed, then took another ten out of an envelope. I closed the wallet and then put it away. "Who's got a safe place to put this for the bike ride?" I asked.

Just then we heard the Taylors' back door open. My heart leaped! Matt! But it wasn't. It was Emma's oldest (and some say cutest, but not me) brother, Sam.

"Hey, Cupcakers," he said, throwing his backpack into his locker in the mudroom. (Yes, the Taylors have lockers, just like at school.) He took off his baseball cap, running his fingers through his wavy blond hair.

"Hi, Sam!" said Mia and Katie in unison, all perky. They love him. Mia batted her eyelashes at him, and Katie grinned a megawatt smile.

Emma's eyes narrowed with a plan. "Sammy? Could you take us to the Quickie Mart to get some bacon? Please, please, please? It would save us so much time!"

Sam was pulling food out of the fridge to make a salad or a huge hero or something. All the Taylor boys do is eat, I swear! He looked down at his ingredients, then he said, "I guess so. I could probably use some more mayo. Will you save me some cupcakes as payment?" he asked, his bright blue eyes twinkling.

Katie and Mia couldn't promise him fast enough. "Then let's go!" he said.

Being annoyed with everyone and having just arrived, I really didn't feel like going. Emma had to go, because it was her brother taking them. And Mia and Katie would not miss an opportunity to be seen driving anywhere with Sam Taylor, even if it was only on a bacon errand.

"I'll just stay here and start the batter," I said.

"Okay. Be right back!" called Emma.

I know the Taylors' kitchen as well as I know my own. I could reasonably show up and prepare a three-course meal there without anyone batting an eye, so I felt totally comfortable being left there by myself, especially knowing no one else was due back for a while. I turned on the TV to watch a rerun of my favorite dancing show, *Celebrity Ballroom*, and I quickly whipped up the batter in Emma's pride and joy: her pink KitchenAid stand mixer. I then ladled the batter into the cupcake liners that Emma had on hand. We were only making four dozen cupcakes today, so it was pretty fast and easy. When I'd finished, I put them in the oven and then began to wash the dishes, turning up the TV volume to hear over the water.

Between the hiss of the water from the faucet and the dance music blaring out of the TV, I didn't hear anyone come in. So when I heard someone call my name right beside me, I screamed and jumped about ten feet in the air.

"Sorry!" said Matt, hands in the air, backing away. "I didn't mean to scare you!"

I turned off the water and stood there shaking, my wet hands over my heart, which was pounding.

"TV's a little loud too, don't you think?" he asked, laughing as he turned down the volume.

"You scared me to death!" I said. I hate being scared. It always makes me feel cranky afterward. Somehow, today my annoyance negated my usual nervousness around Matt. I only felt mad.

"Smells good in here," said Matt, sniffing appreciatively.

I nodded. "Book club job," I said. "Caramel and bacon."

"Oh, those are one of my favorites! I love that bacon-caramel combo! Are you going to have any extras?" he asked hopefully.

Between the disorganized club members (not me) and the terrifying scare I'd just had, I was not in a nice mood. "Well, we already have to give some to Sam for driving to the Quickie Mart to buy bacon. I don't know how many they promised him, but we can't just keep giving away our profits like this . . . ," I said without thinking.

"Oh, hey, no problem. Sorry. I wouldn't want to eat up all your profits . . . ," said Matt, and he turned to leave the room.

Oh no. I suddenly realized I'd just been really mean. After all, there I was, taking over his kitchen, without his sister even being there, baking with his family's supplies, saying his brother could have some cupcakes but he couldn't. And worst of all, I was not being cool. I was caring way too much and being uptight and definitely not being a free spirit.

"Wait! Sorry! I'm sorry, Matt. That was really rude. I just . . . of course you can have some cupcakes. I love that you love them!" Ugh. Did I really just say that? Uncool!

"No, I get it. I totally understand. You guys are trying to run a business, so . . . that's chill. I'm just going to finish a design I've been working on. Later!" And he left the room.

I sat down heavily in a chair. *Why am I such a dork?* I thought, staring into space. *Why can I not know the right things to say or do at the right times?* Callie would have immediately turned that whole thing into a major flirt session. She would have said, *For you, Matt, anything! I'll save you the best ones, with extra bacon!* Then she would have flipped her hair and smiled a big sparkly smile at him. I, on the other hand, squashed all of Matt's friendliness and enthusiasm, turned him down, and barked at him in his own home.

I wanted to die.

CHAPTER 9

The CEO in the FBLA

$\mathcal{M}$att didn't come downstairs again before I left that Friday. I told the others sort of vaguely what had happened, and I set aside three cupcakes on a plate for Matt, kicking in three of my own dollars to make up for it. I felt awful.

The next morning, as I headed to Emma's to bake for the swim meet, I half hoped I'd see him and half feared it. Luckily, he was at cross-country practice when we arrived, and I was quickly swept up in all the work that needed to be done.

After thinking over the options on unit price, I'd decided we just needed to make the cupcakes a little smaller than usual. Instead of filling each wrapper three-quarters of the way with batter, we'd just fill them halfway, leaving us with cakes that were level with the tops of the wrappers once they were baked, rather than puffing into big, muffinlike crowns.

Mia was willing to agree to anything to redeem herself, and Emma and Katie were fine with the somewhat skimpy cupcakes.

"Never again, though!" I said as we filled the cupcake wrappers.

"Never!" promised the others.

Then Katie spoke up: "Alexis, um, we've been talking about it and . . . we think the Cupcake Club runs a lot better when you're in charge."

I looked up in surprise. Emma and Mia were nodding.

"We know it's a lot of work for you . . . ," Emma added.

"Actually, I don't know how you fit it all in!" said Mia.

"But we'd like to ask you to officially be our CEO," Katie finished.

"The boss!" said Emma, laughing.

"We really can't do it unless you run it," said Mia.

Of course I was thrilled to receive such acknowledgment. But I wasn't willing to accept so easily.

"Thanks," I said. "That's really nice. I do love it.

For me, it's as fun as . . . fashion design is for Mia! It's just, it does take a lot of time. And I hate always being the bad guy, the taskmaster."

The other girls were quiet while we filled cupcake wrappers and mixed frosting and thought about it.

"Maybe we need some flow charts or something. Like a company structure, where each of us has the same job all the time and we know how it needs to be done and when, and on a regular basis," suggested Mia.

"Yeah. It's too bad we can't send you to business school, Alexis!" Katie joked.

"I wish!" I said. But then suddenly, I thought of the FBLA. "Actually . . . Mr. Donnelly invited me to join the Future Business Leaders of America at school," I said. I felt like I was bragging by telling them. I was also nervous they'd think I was taking all the credit for the club or, worse, that it was too dorky to even consider doing. I regretted my words as soon as they left my mouth.

But I wasn't expecting the reactions I got!

Mia was so impressed. She said a high school girl who interned for her mom last summer had been a member of the FBLA in middle school, and that was where the girl learned everything she knew about business—and she knew a lot. Emma thought it was an honor to be asked. And Katie said, "I think I'm speaking for all of us when I say, first of all, congratulations. And second of all, it would be an honor to have you represent the Cupcake Club! You deserve it!"

We hadn't heard Matt come in (that guy sure is quiet). But suddenly he was there, saying, "Who's being congratulated? And who's representing the Cupcake Club in what?"

He sat at the kitchen table and began to pull off his sneakers, his light hair sweaty and matted, his dimples appearing in his cheeks as he grimaced. He looked gorgeous and strong and fit.

"Ew! Get out of here, Stinky!" said Emma.

"No, Emma, it's fine!" I said, quick to defend Matt.

"We were just congratulating Alexis," said Mia. "She's—"

"It's nothing," I interrupted. Dylan's words about social death floated through my mind. Could I join the FBLA and keep it a secret?

But Katie wouldn't be hushed. "Alexis was asked by Mr. Donnelly to join the Future Business Leaders of America at school! Isn't that great?"

I wanted to die. There was no flow to go with,

no way to act cool. Matt now knew for sure that I was a dork. It was curtains for me. I couldn't even look up.

"Wait, is that the thing where you get to go to the conference in the city at the end of the year?" asked Matt.

I looked at him and nodded miserably, bracing myself for a snide comment.

But instead Matt said, "Wow! That is so cool! Will you tell me if you learn anything I can use for my graphic design business?" Matt designs things on the computer for people (including the Cupcake Club), like flyers, signs, campaign posters—stuff like that.

At first I thought he might be teasing me, but he wasn't even smiling. He was dead serious. "Sure," I said.

"It's gonna be so interesting. You're lucky!" Matt got up and then walked into the mudroom. He flipped his sneakers into his locker, then went to wash his hands.

"And thanks for the cupcakes last night, Alexis. You didn't need to do that," he said, his back to me as he stood at the sink. I couldn't see his face.

I quickly looked at Emma. She shrugged and smiled. So she must've told him they were from me.

"Oh, no problem. I just . . . I know you like them so . . ." I tried to channel Callie and the other PGCs. It didn't feel right, but I went for it. "I made those especially for you, with extra bacon. I hope they were okay!" I blushed. I couldn't believe I'd been so flirty.

Matt turned around with a big smile on his face. "Thanks. Any more today?"

"No!" interrupted Mia. "Alexis is being very stern about our unit price and our markup. If we give any of the swim team's cupcakes away, the boss lady is going to dock our pay," she teased.

But I was mortified. "Oh, come on. Surely we could spare a couple of cupcakes for Matt!"

"Uh-uh. You said so!" said Katie. "Sorry, pal!"

But luckily Matt was laughing. "How much profit would I be eating if I had one?"

Everyone looked at me expectantly. I couldn't help myself. I quickly did the calculations in my head. "One dollar's worth. Or about three percent. It's fine, though," I insisted. "I'll cover it for the swim team."

"Nope! Every penny counts! Especially for future business leaders! Hey, maybe you should go as Donald Trump for the costume parade!" Matt cackled.

I froze. Matt had mentioned the parade. Here was my big opening! But could I really ask him on a date in front of all these people, including his own sister, my best friend? I thought of Dylan and all her advice. *Don't be too accessible* and *Have a good guy friend* were kind of canceling each other out right here. I knew she'd want me to march with Matt. But would it be cool if *I* asked *him*? Not so much.

While I stood there thinking, Emma piped up, "What are you doing for the parade, Matty?"

"Ah, you know I hate that stuff, I'm not going," he said, turning away to grab a bag by the door.

What?!

Luckily, Emma wasn't going to let him get away with that. "You can't hate it! It's a rite of passage! You've got to go!"

"Nah," he said. "Not for me. See ya!" And he left the room to go upstairs.

I looked at Emma after he left. I was aghast. "What do we do now?" I asked.

"I was waiting for you to ask him!" she said.

"Why should I ask him? You should have asked him! He's your brother!"

"Exactly! And if I do the asking, he'll say no. It's got to be you!"

"Why is this so hard?" I wailed, and covered my face.

Just then the timer went off for the first batches of cupcakes, and we had to get the next ones in. Time was ticking away. I snapped into action. Anything to distract myself from yet another missed opportunity. We flipped the cupcakes out onto the cooling racks and began filling the cupcake pans with new liners, being careful not to burn ourselves on the metal trays. It wasn't until I started ladling in the batter that something occurred to me.

"Emma," I said quietly. "If Matt isn't going to the pep rally parade, then Callie doesn't have a chance. Even if she does ask."

Emma looked at me like I was an idiot. "First of all, that doesn't solve any of our problems. We still have no one to march with. Second of all, don't you know he's just saying that? He's either too shy or too lazy to ask someone himself. But you can bet if someone asks him, he'll say yes."

Huh. "I guess you really do know boys," I said.

"Occupational hazard," Emma said with a shrug. "But I had another idea. I think you should ask him if he and Joe Fraser want to walk with you and me. Then it's like a group thing and not so date-y, which I know bothers you."

"It doesn't bother me. I just . . . I'm nervous, that's all."

"Well, the next time you see him, you have to ask him, okay?" she said. "It's only a week away, and I know for sure he doesn't have a costume of any sort. We can't let that become an excuse for him to not go. Okay? Pinkie promise?"

Ugh. I hate to pinkie promise, because then it means I have to do whatever dreaded thing I've promised to do. "Fine," I said, irritated. "Now let's focus on this swim team thing!"

CHAPTER 10

Take a Dive

*I*t felt good to be back in business, especially in the driver's seat. I ran the rest of our morning like a drill sergeant, but a nice drill sergeant. I tried not to be bossy, and the others tried not to mind when I was.

We got the bacon cupcakes assembled and delivered to the book club. Then we rushed back to the Taylors' to frost and pack the swim team cupcakes. At the last minute I grabbed the extra frosting and a bunch of plastic knives, and stuck them in my insulated tote bag. You never know.

Mia's stepbrother, Dan, picked us up in her mom's Mini Cooper, to give us a ride to the town's pool, where the meet was being held. It was pretty tricky fitting all us girls and all those cupcakes into the car. Suddenly (with visions of cupcakes splattered on the pavement) I called my dad and asked him to come in the Suburban. I sent the other three ahead with the first load and took three cupcake carriers and waited for my dad on the Taylors' driveway.

My dad pulled up quickly, and we loaded the Suburban and safely stowed the cupcakes, then headed out to the town's pool.

"Any extras?" my dad asked hopefully. My mom keeps us on a major health-food diet, so my dad is always looking for any little crumb of junk food he can get his hands on.

"Sorry, Dad, not today," I said. "It would be bad business. Our margins are too tight as it is. I'll make another batch soon, though, and save you some," I said, thinking of Matt.

"Hey, I meant to ask you, what did you ever decide to do about that business club at school?" he said, taking his eyes off the road to glance sideways at me.

I looked away, staring out the window. "Oh, I don't know. I'm not sure it's for me . . . ," I said. But I thought of Matt's reaction as I said it.

"Listen, sweetheart, I think you should go for

it. Don't listen to Dylan. It would be a wonderful experience for you," he said.

"It would officially make me a dork," I said. "With no hope of ever being considered cool."

"That's ridiculous. Being cool is a state of mind. As long as you're cool with who you are, you'll be fine," he said.

"Easy for you to say," I said.

"Well, you're right. But it's much more important to follow your passions and to be true to yourself. I mean look at all the people who didn't follow convention and who went on to do great things. Innovators, like Steve Jobs, Bill Gates, Jim Henson . . ."

"I know, I know," I said.

"The list of leaders is endless. And it's cool to lead. It's not cool to follow, to do what other people tell you to, or what you think other people think you should do. Does that make sense?"

"I guess. But Dylan . . ."

"Look at Dylan! A perfect example," said my dad. "Do you see her following anyone?"

I shook my head. "No. I guess not."

"So, there you go. Why should you follow her? Or anyone? Just follow your heart, follow your passions. Go for what excites you!" he said.

We pulled into the parking lot and then jumped out to get the cupcakes.

"Thanks for saving the day, Dad," I said, and I gave him a big hug.

"Anytime!" he said, kissing the top of my head.

Inside, it was hot and humid, just as I'd suspected. I reached the table where the other girls had been directed to set up the cupcakes, and I found them in a panic.

"Alexis! Thank goodness you're here! Look!" cried Mia.

She had arranged the cupcakes in a wave design, just as she'd planned. The pale blue frosting was pretty, and it did look kind of like a wave. Except for one thing. All the icing was sliding off the cupcakes from the heat.

"Oh," I said. "Okay. Well . . . let me think."

Emma stood there wringing her hands while Katie bit her lip and Mia hyperventilated. I looked around the room. It was starting to fill up. We didn't have time to go home and rethink this. I watched a kid dive off a diving board into the water, his hands slicing the surface, but his body leaving not a ripple on the water. Pretty amazing, those divers, headfirst . . .

"I've got it!" I said suddenly, snapping my fingers as it came to me. I began calling out orders.

"Emma, we have to get Matt to do a quick poster for us, in bright blues and greens. Just type. It needs to say, 'Take a Dive with the Swim Team's Cupcakes!' Okay? Can you call him and ask him to do that for us? He can put a credit and contact info for his company at the bottom of the sign. Tell him. He just needs to get it over here in the next . . . oh . . . half hour. Okay?"

Emma nodded, flipping open her phone.

"Mia and Katie, you're not going to like this, but bear with me . . ." I explained my plan.

Matt arrived, breathless, twenty-five minutes later, with three copies of an awesome poster for us to hang around the table. It said what we'd asked, but he'd figured out a way for the words to be splashing into water, with little droplets flinging off the letters, all green and blue.

"Oh, Matt, it's amazing! You're a genius!" I said. And I wasn't even hamming it up or flirting like Callie would have. I meant it! He actually blushed.

"No prob," he said.

He hung up the posters while I instructed the swim team cocaptains who were manning the table on what they'd do to sell the cupcakes.

"Okay, you're going to take the money—three dollars each—and put it into the cash box. Then you're going to pick up a cupcake . . ." We'd arranged them top down on the table, so they were resting on their frosted tops, with their bottoms in the air, still in Mia's original wave design. "Then you grab a knife and scrape the frosting off the platter, then get a little extra frosting from the bowl, and slather it all on top and hand it over. Okay?"

"Awesome!" one of them said.

"This is so cool! How did you ever think of this? It's so clever!" the other one asked.

"It was Mia's idea," I said, gesturing at her.

"No way. It was our boss, Alexis. She thought up the whole thing," protested Mia.

"Well, Matt Taylor did the signs!" I said. "You know what? It was a team effort!"

"A team effort for a team effort!" said Katie, and we all laughed.

"Let me be the first to buy a couple!" I said. I handed over six dollars and then gave the finished cupcakes to Matt.

"Thanks!" he said, surprised. "You didn't need to do that!"

"It's the least I could do after you saved the day like that for us."

"It sounds like you're the one who saved the day, actually. Here, I can't eat them both right now. Why don't you have one?"

I shrugged and took the cupcake from his hand. "Thanks."

"Cheers," he said, and he tapped his cupcake against mine.

"Cheers," I said back. I took a deep breath and decided to go for it. "Matt . . ."

I swear I was about to ask him to march with me right then when who should be walking up to us but Sydney, Callie, and Bella from the PGC. I didn't know Sydney and Callie were on the swim team, but they must've been. They were wearing bikini tops and short shorts with flip-flops, and Sydney was carrying pom-poms.

"Hey, Matt!" they singsonged as they walked up to him.

"Hey," he said, licking off frosting from his lip.

"Wow! Look at those cupcakes!" said Callie eagerly.

"Yeah, talk about fattening," said Sydney as I smushed my final, slightly too-large bite into my mouth. Whoops.

"Look at these cool posters," said Bella. "The letters are all drippy. It would be cool to do it in red, like vampire blood."

Sydney rolled her eyes. "Not everything in life comes back to vampires, Bella," she said.

I had finished chewing and was just standing there like an idiot, but I wasn't about to walk away from Matt and leave him to the wolves. I turned to Callie.

"I didn't know you guys are on the swim team," I said.

Callie looked at me, confused. "What?"

I gestured to her bathing suit and Sydney's. "I didn't realize you two were on the swim team."

Callie looked embarrassed. "Oh, we're not. We just . . . got dressed up to support the team, right, Sydney?" She kind of tried to laugh it off.

Sydney gave her a haughty look. "Yeah. The girls' swim team is for dorks. But we like coming to see the boys in their bathing suits. And we didn't want them to feel self-conscious, so we decided to turn it into a pool party! Right, girls?" She squealed and waved her pom-poms in the air.

"Buy a cupcake to support the team?" said one of the cocaptains, noting Sydney was a fan.

"Sure!" said Callie, reaching into her shorts pocket.

But Sydney stopped her by grabbing her arm. "No, thanks! Bikinis and cupcakes don't mix!"

Callie looked disappointed, but Sydney said, "We want to make sure we fit into our fairy outfits for the *pep rally parade*." She glared at Callie as she said it.

Callie blushed and then shook her head a tiny bit and looked down at the floor.

Sydney sighed in aggravation. "I have to do everything myself around here," she said.

I knew how she felt, but I wasn't exactly sympathetic. I knew things were about to spiral out of control. My control. I knew I should go with the flow, play it cool, be a free spirit, not be seen to care too much. But how do you get anything you want in life if you act like that? That's what I want to know. I steeled myself for what was coming next, and all the while my brain was racing to see if I could figure out how to get Matt away from the PGC and then invite him to march with me.

"What are you being for the parade, Matty?" asked Sydney, all flirty.

"Oh . . . I'm not . . ."

I knew what he was about to say, and I weighed

the risk of social ruin (the PGC finding out Dylan had lied about my parade plans) against mortification (inviting Matt in front of these girls), and I just blurted out the first thing that came to my mind.

"He's being a Greek god," I said. "He's marching with me." I couldn't even look at him as I said it. I just prayed he'd go along with it.

I could see him turn to me in surprise, and now I needed to cover for that. I looked at him. "You hadn't heard what our final costume plan was. Now I ruined the surprise! Silly me!" I said, and I laughed, all flirty. *Get me out of here, get me out of here,* I thought.

Matt was looking at me in confusion. Sydney looked mad, and Callie still looked embarrassed.

I pressed on. *If you're going to go down, at least go down in flames,* I thought. I said to Matt, "I know, I know, you didn't know what Emma and I had cooked up for you and Joe to wear when you marched with us. But failing to plan is planning to fail! That's one of my mottoes."

Finally, a big grin spread across Matt's face. "Whatever you say, boss," he said, chuckling.

Boss? I fake laughed. "Ha-ha. I'm not anyone's boss."

Luckily, the swim team coach chose that

moment to get on the bullhorn and announce the cupcake sale. The table was stormed, and Matt and I got jostled out of the way and separated from the PGC. As my adrenaline wore off, my knees started to shake when I realized what I'd done. *Oh my goodness!* I thought. I needed to cover my tracks.

I turned to Matt and said weakly, "Hey, so, I'm sorry about that back there. I just . . ."

He was smiling, though. "Thanks. You saved me from looking like a major dork for not having any plans. I appreciate it. That was funny. Greek gods. Quick thinking!"

Wait, did he not realize I had actually just invited him? He thought that was just a joke? Like a bail out? What could I say? What should I do? If I told him I'd been serious, would I look like a major dork? I decided to go with the flow.

"Oh, yeah. Anytime. So . . . I guess . . . I mean, were you planning on going with them and I just messed it all up?" I asked. *Please say no, please say no,* I chanted in my head.

"No. Those girls are too much. I mean, Callie's fine, but Sydney is torture. She's so aggressive and bossy."

Bossy? "Is bossy bad?" I asked, thinking how he'd just called me "boss" and also seeing as how

I was the boss of the Cupcake Club.

"Well, yeah. Who wants to be bossed around?"

"Yeah. No one, I guess," I said. *Callie's fine* was floating in my head. *Is that a good "fine" or just an okay "fine"?* I wanted to ask, but that wouldn't be going with the flow, either.

Mia, Katie, and Emma appeared at our side. "Should we go?" asked Mia.

"I guess," said Emma. Turning to me, she asked, "What do you say, boss?"

"I am not the boss!" I said. It came out a little more forcefully than I had meant it to. Emma jumped and looked surprised.

"Okay! Sorry! I get it!" she said.

I rolled my eyes.

"Let's go," said Katie. "Alexis, is your dad coming back?"

I looked at my watch. "Yup. He should be here by now. He can drive us all. Let's get the cupcake carriers and head out."

"So, I guess you guys aren't staying for the meet . . . ," Matt said.

"Matt, thanks so much for your help," I said, all businesslike.

"No prob. Glad to be of service. Thanks for the cupcake," he said. Then he added, "And . . . for saving me." He hesitated a minute. It looked like he was going to say something else or ask me something. But then it seemed as if he changed his mind. "Anyway . . ."

I looked at him. "Okay, then," I said finally, going with the flow. "Thanks for the awesome posters."

"Bye."

"Bye," I said, and walked away.

CHAPTER 11

Greek Goddesses and Friends

That night, as I sat in my room—working on flow charts for the Cupcake Club, but actually thinking only about Matt and my bungling of the invitation today—there was a knock on my door.

"Come in," I said.

It was Dylan. "Dad says I have to tell you to stop worrying about being cool," she said with absolutely no animation or enthusiasm. Then she continued in a monotone voice as she took a seat on my bed. "I'm supposed to say it doesn't matter, follow your dreams."

I spun around in my desk chair to face her, put my fingertips together, and looked at Dylan. "Wow. You're doing a really convincing job," I said, echoing her monotone.

She smiled, then she sighed and began to speak normally. "Listen, just for the record, you're the one who wanted my help. It's not like I grabbed you and said, 'You're a dork. Let me help' or anything like that. Make sure Dad knows that, because it doesn't seem like he does."

"Okay," I said, nodding at her. "But just explain this to me: How is it that going with the flow makes such a mess of everything? It seems like it should be the opposite."

"I'm not answering any more questions. It only gets me into trouble," said Dylan, examining her nails.

"Come on, Dylly, just this last one!" I protested.

Dylan sighed heavily. "Look, I'm not an expert. I just know what I see. I'm starting to think maybe there are different kinds of cool. There's, like, 'leader cool,' where you do everything a little ahead of everyone else, and then there's, like, 'renegade cool,' where you just march to your own drummer. I guess I should have been a little clearer on that. I'm thinking you probably fall more into the renegade category, since you're not a cookie-cutter type of person."

"Oh great. I'm a weirdo," I said. "I knew it."

"No! Stop. You're not at all. You're just . . . You

have interests that are a little outside the norm for people your age. But that doesn't mean they're bad. It's just, if you're going to take a chance on them, you have to go for it, whole hog. Don't just do it halfway, you know? Like, if you're going to do the Cupcake Club, then go all out: run it, be a serious CEO, join the FBLA, read business books—whatever. Go for what you want. That's what is cool. Not doing it is dorky, and doing something only halfway . . . well, that's not really cool at all. It's just kind of lame. Do you get it?"

"I guess so," I said.

Dylan got mad then. "Don't tell Dad I gave you more advice on coolness, though, okay?"

"Okay! I won't! I already swore I wouldn't!"

Dylan stood up, satisfied with my answer.

First thing Sunday morning, Mia called me, all excited. "Come over! My mom got the costumes back from Hector! We need to try them on! The others are coming with their stuff too, and my mom's going to help us style them. Bring the sandals, okay?"

I had my mom drive me over to Mia's in a flash. Emma was already there, and Katie arrived soon after.

Mrs. Valdes took my dress and Mia's out of black garment bags and laid them out on the sofas in the living room.

"Wow!" Emma exclaimed breathlessly. "That's gorgeous, Alexis."

I leaned in to finger the soft material. Hector had added rectangular jeweled clasps to the shoulders, bunching the material so that it gathered in tiny pleats at the top, then draped down across the front in a graceful arc. I couldn't wait to try it on.

"Okay, *mis amores*, run and get into your costumes and then meet me in my room. We'll go through one by one and accessorize you!" Mrs. Valdes said.

We spent the next hour and a half playing fashion show, with Mrs. Valdes raiding her closet and trying things on us to enhance our outfits. Emma wound up looking amazing in her hippie costume. Mrs. Valdes added a hairpiece called a "fall" to her hair that made it look really long, then she lent Emma a suede fringed vest to go over the bell bottoms and tie-dyed shirt Emma had brought. Mia had a pair of platform boots that fit Emma perfectly, and they dug out a pair of round tinted glasses of Dan's to complete the look.

Next up was Katie, the genie. She had a pair of culottes and a long-sleeved shirt with a scarf to wrap around her head. Mrs. Valdes swapped out her shirt for this flowy, white one with billowy arms, and wrapped a gold lamé scarf around her middle as a belt. Then she took a little pillbox hat and attached Katie's head scarf to it, so it flowed down the back. Finally, she produced a pair of shoes from Tibet that curled up into pointy toes and looked magical. Mia gave Katie an anklet made up of tiny bells, which would jingle as she walked. She looked unbelievable!

I went next, and I was so psyched with how my dress came out. It was soft, it fit perfectly, and it was sooo comfortable, like liquid swirling around me. I strapped on my tie-up gold Roman sandals. Mrs. Valdes put my hair up into this loose bun and then pinned it, sticking little silk leaves all around my head. Then she put a garland of silk leaves around my waist, so it looked like a belt.

"And now for the finishing touch!" she said. I watched as she ran over to her jewelry box on her dressing table and pulled out the gold knot earrings she'd had on that day at Icon. She held them up and crossed back to clip them onto my ears.

"Oh, Mrs. Valdes. I can't wear these! What if I lose one?" I protested.

"I know you, Alexis, and you won't lose one. But even if you did, it's okay. I got them for fifteen dollars at H&M last year. They are temporary by nature. Now turn around, and let's see the full effect."

I spun in place, and everyone cheered. "Oh, I wish Dylan were here to see you!" Mrs. Valdes said as she clapped her hands.

"Me too!" I agreed. "She'll be so jealous when she finds out we raided your closet without her."

Mia went last, and her costume was the simplest but the best of all, just because it took kind of a standard idea (witch—black dress, black hat, black shoes) and made it so glamorous. Her dress had scraps of floaty black tulle sewn on that flitted and flicked as she moved. There were little sequins hidden here and there to catch your eye amid all the black. Her hat was very, very tall and very, very pointy—almost kind of kooky-looking, but chic. And her shoes were superhigh heels with superpointy toes and bursts of tulle pointing off the toes and heels, like a little shoe Mohawk. Mia's mom gave her tons of silvery necklaces and jangly silver bracelets to wear, so she made a tinkly noise as she moved.

"Wow, Mia! You look beautiful!" I said. We all agreed. Her costume was fantastic!

Mrs. Valdes ran to get her camera, since she wasn't sure where we'd all be dressing for the parade next weekend.

"I'm so glad we're not fairies," said Katie.

"I know. Also, I think it's cooler that we're not all matchy, matchy. It's kind of babyish to go in a big group theme," said Emma.

"What are your partners being?" I asked Katie and Mia, thinking of Matt.

"Chris is a warlock," said Mia. "I helped him with the costume." She smiled. "It was fun."

Katie laughed. "I convinced George to be an astronaut like on the TV show, so he's going for it! His dad was going to help him make the costume. He's going to wear a bubble helmet and everything!"

"Fun!" I said. But I was feeling a little wistful. I wish I had had the guts to tell Matt I'd really been serious yesterday. I shouldn't have gone with the flow.

Emma and I avoided eye contact. We hadn't recently discussed going with Matt and Joe. But now that I had this great costume, I really wanted to march with Matt. I didn't want to waste it.

"Going with the flow doesn't get you what you want in life," I said out loud.

The others looked at me strangely.

"Of course not, silly!" said Katie. "Only limp noodles go with the flow!"

I giggled. "That sounds so appetizing. Like something a witch would make!"

Mia cackled. "Heh, heh, heh, my pretties! Who would like some limp noodle pie?"

We all started acting out our costume characters as Mrs. Valdes came back into the room with her camera. We hammed it up in all sorts of shots, and then reluctantly took everything off. It had been fun. And now I knew I had to get up the nerve to ask Matt. No more limp noodle pie for me!

CHAPTER 12

Carpe Diem—Seize the Day!

I knew all the teachers would be back at school Monday, getting everything ready for the new school year. So I called and left Mr. Donnelly a message. He called me back a few minutes later.

"Hi! Mr. Donnelly! Am I too late?" I asked.

"Hello, Alexis. I'm assuming you mean the Future Business Leaders of America? No, you're not too late. I was taking a calculated risk that you wouldn't take so long to think about it and then say no." He laughed. "So shall I write the letter?"

"Yes, please. And is there anything I need to do on my end?"

"You'll need to pull together a résumé. . . . I can e-mail you some samples. And then just write a one-paragraph essay on why you want to join and what your focus will be. Can you have it to me by Wednesday?" he asked.

I nodded. "I can have it to you by tomorrow."

"Even better! Great!"

That night, my mom helped me put together a really good résumé that listed all my business experience (babysitting, Cupcake Club, running bake sales at school, selling Girl Scout cookies when I was younger—stuff like that). I listed my areas of responsibility in the Cupcake Club, including the financial planning I do, along with the marketing ideas I'd had for Emma's dog-walking business, and a few other things.

Then it was time to write my paragraph. I sat at my desk and then cracked my knuckles. I'm better at math than writing, so I always have a hard time getting started. The clock ticked, and I shifted in my seat. Finally, I caved.

"Dad!" I yelled.

For the next fifteen minutes, my dad and I brainstormed, talking about what I enjoyed most in business and where I felt I needed to grow. I took notes and jotted down key words as we talked, and when he left, I felt energized. I knew what I wanted to say, and here's what I wrote:

My name is Alexis Becker. My business experience to date has been customer driven and marketing oriented, mainly in the food service industry, and now I'd like to take it to the next level. If I were accepted into the Future Business Leaders of America, my focus would be on innovations in leadership. I would like to learn how to better lead employees by inspiring them to be creative and by empowering them to work independently. I do not want to be a micromanager. I would also like to learn how to lead in my industry, developing new products before my competitors and finding new ways to reach customers through marketing. I would appreciate the opportunity to harness my enthusiasm and passions and turn them into action—to just go for it, to never hold back, and to learn how to lead by example. Thank you for your consideration of my application.

I thought it was pretty good, and my parents liked it too. Even Dylan, who was passing by as I read it aloud to them, gave me a thumbs-up. I felt great. I printed out the final copy and put it in an envelope to deliver to Mr. Donnelly the next day.

After finishing the letter, I wrapped up some Cupcake business, and it was still kind of early. There was something I needed to do, and it was on my mind. I just wouldn't feel settled until I did it. I thought of my own words from the FBLA paragraph. How I wanted to go for it and to never hold back. How I wanted to lead by example.

I can do this, I can do this, I told myself.

I took a deep breath, and I punched the familiar sequence of numbers into the phone.

"Hello?" asked a familiar voice.

"Emma, it's me, Alexis," I said.

"Oh hi! I was going to call you! When are we getting together to bake for the retirement party this weekend?"

"I just e-mailed everyone about that," I said. "It should be in your in-box. But we'll do it at Katie's first thing on Saturday, so we can get ready for the parade by three o'clock, okay?"

"Perfect. Anything else going on?" She was obviously looking to chat, but I didn't have time. I'd lose momentum.

I cringed. "Actually, I wonder if I could speak to Matt?"

There was a pause, then Emma said, "Oh. Right. Sure. Hang on. I'll get him."

The phone clunked on the table. I could just picture the upstairs hallway and Emma walking to Matt's room. I had kind of an unfair advantage in all this, in that I'd been to Matt's so many times and was so comfortable with his whole family. *Why should I be nervous, anyway?* I thought. *Why don't I just pretend I'm the CEO of a big company making a sales call. CEOs never take no for an answer!*

"Hello?" His scratchy, deepish voice startled me.

"Hey, Matt, it's Alexis." I gulped. I didn't feel so CEO-ish anymore. *Go with the flow,* I started to tell myself. But no! There's no flow anymore. *Carpe diem!* I reminded myself. *Seize the day!* That's better.

"Hey. How's it going?" he asked.

"Good. Listen, I'm just going to cut to the chase. . . ."

I could hear Dylan's advice in my head. *Go for what you want. That's what is cool. Not doing it is dorky.* I thought of making this into a big group invitation thing. I thought of inviting him and Joe to join me and Emma as a foursome. But then I thought about what I really wanted, what my own goal was: I wanted to march with Matt Taylor in the parade, darn it!

"Would you like to come march with me in the parade on Saturday?" I said it in one really quick rush. I guess it came out a little too fast, because Matt didn't catch it.

"What?" he asked.

I took another deep breath, dying that I had to say it all again. "The parade. Would you like to march with me on Saturday?"

There was a pause. I could hear the wheels turning in his mind as he struggled to find an answer, a gentle way to say no, to turn me down. I cringed and closed my eyes.

"Sure. Thanks," he said. "What do I need to wear?"

What?!

YAHOO!

Now I wasn't sure what to say, so I started to ramble a little. "Um, well, I actually am going as a Greek goddess. I wasn't kidding about that. You can wear whatever you want. Or you could be a Greek god and wear a toga. Like a white sheet, you know?"

"Oh yeah. Sam knows how to do that. His friend had a toga party last year. I could do that."

"Really? Oh, that's so great!" I said. I didn't want to sound dorky or overly enthusiastic, but this was turning out fantastically. Success made me generous. "Also, listen, Emma might need someone to walk with too. I don't know if she's talked to you about it or not, but . . ." I was just totally going for it now, covering all my bases.

Matt replied, "Well, I could bring Joe. I don't think he has a plan. We were just going to bail on the parade and go to the pep rally and bonfire, so . . . I'm sure he'd be happy to march. Should he wear a toga too?"

"Um, maybe he should be a hippie," I said. "That's what Emma's dressing up as, and she looks great."

"Cool. Okay. So we'll just meet you . . ."

"There. We'll meet at your house on Saturday, and we can all go over together. How's that?"

"Great. Sounds like a plan! Thanks," he said. I could tell by his voice that he really *was* happy about it. Maybe Emma knew her brother better than I gave her credit for. Maybe he was just too nervous—or too lazy—to ask anyone.

"It'll be fun," I said.

I hung up the phone and sat at my desk, staring at it with a huge, dorky smile on my face. I didn't care if I wasn't cool. I was sure I was the happiest girl in America right then. I'd gone for what I wanted and gotten it! And I'd hooked Emma up at the same time!

I went down the hall to Dylan's room in a trance. "You're fired," I said, walking in without knocking.

"What?" asked Dylan, looking up from her book in confusion.

"Your work is done," I said. "I'm cool."

Dylan rolled her eyes. "You can't fire me. I already quit," she said, and she turned back to her book.

"Either way," I said. "Mission accomplished."

CHAPTER 13

My Perfect Day

$\mathcal{S}$aturday was beautiful: a perfectly warm summer day, but there was a hint of fall in the air too. We were at Katie's bright and early, chatting about the parade route and whether we'd be cold in our costumes since the temperature was supposed to drop that night. Dylan had told me that kids in the past have gone to the stadium in advance to drop off bags with jackets and sweaters and stuff to save seats. I thought that was a pretty cool way to plan ahead, and I suggested we do that. Everyone loved the idea.

"How about the boys?" asked Emma. "Should we call and tell them too?"

"Well . . ." Not if I had to do the calling.

"Come on," said Emma. "It's not fair to them. They'll be freezing, and we'll be warm and toasty."

"Oh! I bet I could get Dan to lend me his jacket that would work great with Chris's costume. I'm going to call him and Chris right now!" said Mia.

"Alexis, you should call Matt," said Emma sternly.

"Fine," I said. And I did it too.

Lucky for me, he wasn't home, so I left a message with Mrs. Taylor. Phew!

We finished our cinnamon bun cupcakes with cream cheese frosting with plenty of time to spare. Katie's mom had Saturday morning hours at her office, but she was going to give us a ride, with our cupcakes, at twelve, so we had some time to kill.

"Hey, want to watch the last episode of *Celebrity Ballroom*? I DVRed it last night!" said Katie.

Emma and Mia were totally up for it, but I had to step in. "Ladies, let's do a quick meeting and then we can watch the show, okay? We just have some loose ends to tie up."

They moaned a little bit, but it was more for show, and I wasn't having any of it anymore. "If you want to stay in the club, pipe down. I'm toning down my management style, so you have to tone down your worker complaints, okay?" That shut them up fast.

I handed out flow charts that detailed the responsibilities of each person, the general time schedule we worked on, and an overview of the upcoming jobs we had for the next month. I also included a profit-and-loss statement that showed how much the cupcakes cost to bake and how much we could charge for them and how much we'd make. It was all organized by cupcake style, based on ingredients and unit cost.

"Wow, Alexis, this is awesome!" said Katie.

"You've been working really hard!" agreed Mia.

"I have. And the reason is so I don't have to be a nag anymore." I walked them through everything, and because it was laid out so cleanly and so simply, they understood it and were into it. It wasn't just some vague meeting with me nattering on about numbers. Mia had some good ideas about where we could innovate (display, supplying party goods) and where we might spend some of our profits (new platters, a new carrier to replace the one with the broken handle), and Emma made three suggestions for new recipes to try. Katie mentioned she'd seen the fancy vanilla extract we like for way cheaper at Williams-Sonoma, and we decided to take a field trip there the following week to stock up. All in all, it was a very productive meeting in which everyone felt heard and like they contributed.

"Okay? So we're all set," I said, closing my ledger and putting it away in my tote bag.

"Wait, that's it?" said Mia. "Usually we go way longer."

"Nope. Not anymore," I said. "Long, boring meetings are a thing of the past. Now let's go watch that show!"

At four o'clock, my mom dropped me off with my costume at the Taylors'. I was so nervous, I actually rang the doorbell. I felt like I wasn't sure who I was really going there to see.

Mrs. Taylor opened the door. "Alexis, honey! I'm so happy to see you! But why are you ringing the doorbell?"

"Um? I don't know. Practicing for Halloween, I guess!"

She laughed. "Come on in. They're upstairs."

"The Cupcakers? Who else is here already?"

"Oh, you're the first, honey. I meant Matt and Emma. Matt! Emma!" she called. "Alexis is here!"

"Okay! Hi, Alexis!" called Matt from upstairs.

I couldn't help it. I grinned from ear to ear.

"Come on up, Alexis!" yelled Emma.

I went upstairs with my bag, nervous and excited. My stomach was doing flip-flops and my palms were actually sweating. "Hello?" I called.

Matt cracked open his door. "We're in here, getting ready. Emma's in her room. We'll see you soon for the big reveal!" And then he shut the door again. I had to laugh.

"Emma?" I rapped on her door with my knuckles and then went in.

Pretty soon all four of us Cupcakers were there, laughing and playing music and getting ready. But I didn't want it to be too much about us four, so I hustled a little bit in order to get downstairs and meet up with Matt and Joe in the kitchen or TV room. I had heard them go down about ten minutes before we were ready.

"Let's go, girls," I said. They were all putting final dollops of makeup on and tweaking their belts and stuff as they looked in the mirror. Mia had done my hair, and I had dressed myself, carefully slipping on the glorious dress and adjusting my accessories. I had to admit, I looked great. I couldn't wait to see what Matt thought.

"You just want to get downstairs and see your date!" whispered Katie.

"So what if I do?" I laughed. I wasn't going to

hide my happiness or to play it cool. This was the best day of my life so far.

Just then there was a knock on the door. It was Mrs. Taylor. "Alexis, honey, your dad's on the phone."

"Okay, weird, but thanks." The Taylors were driving us over to the stadium in their minivan, so we could drop off our bag of sweaters and jackets, and then us to the start of the parade. I wondered why my dad could be calling.

"Hello?" I said, picking up the phone in the upstairs hallway. I smiled to think this was where Matt had been standing when I asked him out!

"Hi, sweetheart! I just couldn't wait to tell you. Mr. Donnelly called to say the head of the Future Business Leaders of America has accepted your application and that they were very excited about your essay and were looking forward to working with you. He said they don't usually call on the weekends, so he knew they were very impressed. Way to go, Lexi, my love!"

"Yahoo!" I squealed. "Thanks, Dad!"

I hung up the phone and went to tell the others. They were very happy for me, and we finally got downstairs, only moments before we were due to leave.

As I walked down the stairs, I thought about Dylan's advice on not being too friendly, acting like you don't care about stuff, playing it cool. I realized that's just no fun! Why hide your excitement?

As we rounded the corner and went into the kitchen, I saw Matt look up, his eyes searching for me. When they landed on me, they lit up. "Wow! Alexis, you look great!" he said.

"Thanks," I said, smiling. "So do you." And he did.

The parade was amazing, and the pep rally—with all our decorations—was even better. We stayed till the very end. The bonfire smoldered just at the end of the field, and the smell of the wood smoke, mixed with the smell of the popcorn and the hot dogs they were selling, created a delicious aroma I will never forget. It smelled like happiness. (I did make a mental note to approach the concession stand manager about selling cupcakes in the school's colors for the upcoming football games. Life's not all fun and games when there's money to be made!) We ate and cheered for our town's high school's fall sports teams. We had so much fun.

And of course we saw the PGC in their fairy costumes at the parade. Callie and Bella marched

behind Sydney and her date. The outfits had actually turned out well. The girls looked beautiful, but
they were clearly freezing to death. Their costumes
were very light and sleeveless, and it was a bit chilly
even for a summer night.

"Why do some girls think they need to wear so
much makeup?" Matt asked as we walked by.

I shrugged. "I guess they think it makes them
look cool," I said.

"It doesn't," said Matt, stating the obvious. Still,
I was happy to hear it.

I felt Callie's eyes on us as we walked by, and I
felt a little bad. But she did have a chance to invite
Matt, after all, and she never went for it. Anyway, a
part of me wondered if she really even liked him
or if Sydney had just picked him out for her and
bossed her into going for him. It was hard to tell.
Either way, though, I was thrilled to be there—me,
Matt, great costumes, fun night. It all worked out
just right.

"Hey, Alexis!" I heard someone call. It was
Janelle, who was dressed up as a nerd.

I cringed for a second at the thought of
acknowledging her as a friend, right when the
PGC was watching me, but then I pulled myself
together and stopped to chat with her. After all, I

had Matt by my side, so how uncool could I be?

By the end of the night, Chris and Mia were holding hands, and I saw George try to put his arm around Katie, but she swatted him away, laughing. I could feel Matt sneaking sideways glances at me, and it made me feel great. Emma and Joe had fun too, rating people's costumes and throwing popcorn at each other to see if they could catch it in their mouths. They were old friends after all, even though there was no romance there. By the end of the night, when Mr. Taylor came back to pick us up at our assigned meeting place, I didn't want to leave.

We dropped off Mia and then Katie. Chris and George had gotten their own rides home. Joe was sleeping at the Taylors', so he and Emma were still in the car—and Matt, of course—when Mr. Taylor pulled into my driveway.

Matt was sitting in one of the bucket seats next to the sliding door, so he hopped out to let me pass. Or so I thought.

"It's dark, so walk Alexis to the door," said Mr. Taylor.

"I was going to!" Matt said, and he walked me to my back door, which is kind of out of the way, on the other side of the garage.

"That was fun, Alexis. Thanks for inviting me.

I really had never planned on going. I thought it was . . . I don't know. Not such a cool thing to do. But you made it really cool, actually."

I smiled. "Thanks for coming with me. I had a great time too. I'm really glad we all went together too. Next time, I'll bring cupcakes," I said, laughing nervously.

We'd reached the door.

"Well, see you around school. Or, who knows, see you at my house tomorrow probably!" said Matt. And he leaned over and kissed me good-bye, really quickly, on my cheek.

I turned scarlet, but luckily he was already walking really fast down the path back to the car. "Bye!" I called, ecstatically happy. "Thanks!"

I sighed and just enjoyed the moment. Matt Taylor had kind of, sort of kissed me good night. It was absolutely, definitely the coolest thing ever.

Want another sweet cupcake?
Here's a sneak peek
of the ninth book in the

CUPCAKE  DIARIES

series:

Katie

and the

cupcake

war

Mia! Is it really you? I haven't seen you in a gazillion years!" I cried, hugging my friend.

Mia laughed. "Katie, I was only gone for, like, four days," she said.

"That is four days, ninety six hours, or five thousand, seven hundred, and sixty minutes," I said. Then I dramatically put my hand over my heart. "I know, because I counted them all."

"I missed you too," Mia said. "But you couldn't have missed me too much. You were trying out new recipes with the techniques you learned at cooking camp, weren't you?"

"Yes," I told her, "but it felt like you were gone forever. I almost didn't recognize you!"

Actually, I was kidding. Mia looked pretty much

the same, with her straight black hair and dark eyes. She might have gotten a little bit tanner from her long weekend at the beach. She was wearing white shorts and a white tank top with a picture of a pink cupcake on it.

"Hey, I just noticed your shirt!" I said. "That's so cool!"

Mia smiled. "I made it at camp. One of the counselors there was totally into fashion, and she showed me how do this computer thing where you can turn your drawing into a T-shirt design."

I was definitely impressed. "You drew that? It's awesome."

"Thanks," Mia said. "I was thinking maybe I could make T-shirts for the Cupcake Club, for when we go on jobs. You know, so we could all dress alike."

Now it was my turn to laugh. We all like to bake cupcakes, but when it comes to fashion, the members of the Cupcake Club don't have much in common. "Well, I know we all wore matching sweatshirts when we won our first baking contest," I said. "But that was a special occasion. I don't know if you could create one T-shirt we would all be happy wearing on a semi-regular basis."

Then the doorbell rang. It was Emma and

Alexis, and what they were wearing proved my point. Emma is a real "girlie girl," although I don't mean that in a bad way, it just describes Emma really well. Pink is her favorite color, and I don't blame her, because pink looks really nice on you when you have blond hair and blue eyes like Emma does. She had on a pink sundress with tiny white flowers on it and pink flip-flops to match her dress.

Alexis had her curly red hair pulled back in a scrunchie, and she wore a light blue tennis shirt and jean shorts with white sneakers. And I might as well tell you what I was wearing: a yellow T-shirt from my cooking camp signed by all the kids who went there, ripped jeans with iron-on patches, and bare feet, because I was in my house, after all. Oh, and I painted each of my toenails a different color when I was bored.

"Mia! I missed you!" Emma cried, giving Mia a hug.

"So how was your first vacation with your mom, Eddie, and Dan?" Alexis asked. Eddie and Dan are Mia's stepdad and stepbrother, respectively.

"Pretty good," Mia replied. "The beach house was nice, and we got to play a lot of volleyball. But the boardwalk food was terrible."

"That reminds me," I said. "Follow me to the kitchen, guys."

My cooking camp experience had inspired me to surprise my friends for our Cupcake Club meeting. I had covered the kitchen table with my favorite tablecloth, a yellow one with orange and red flowers with green leaves. (Mom says she needs to wear sunglasses to eat when we use it, but I love the bright colors.) Plus, they reminded me of the colors of Mexico and the tablecloth matched all the food I had made.

Laid out on the table was a bowl of bright green guacamole, a platter of enchiladas with red sauce on top, homemade tortilla chips, a pitcher of homemade lemonade, and a plate of tiny cupcakes, each one topped with a dollop of whipped cream and sprinkled with cinnamon.

My friends gasped, and I felt really proud.

"Katie, this looks amazingly fantastic!" Mia said. "Did you make all of this yourself?"

I nodded. "We had Mexican day in cooking camp, and I learned how to do all this stuff," I said. I pointed to the mini cupcakes. "Those are *tres leches* cupcakes."

"Three milks," Mia translated. "Those are sweet and delicious. My *abuela* makes a *tres leches* cake when somebody has a birthday."

I nodded. "Emma, I thought they might be good for the bridal shop."

One of the Cupcake Club's biggest clients is the The Special Day bridal shop. We make mini cupcakes that they give to their customers, and the only requirement is that the frosting has to be white. Emma goes to the bridal shop once a month and helps to give out the cupcakes. She has even modeled the bridesmaids dresses too. (I told you she was a girlie girl.)

"They look perfect!" Emma agreed. "So pretty. And I bet they taste as good as they look."

"Then let's start eating so you can find out," I suggested. "I think the enchiladas are getting cold."

Then my mom walked into the kitchen. She has brown hair, like me, but hers is curly and today it was all messy. She looked tired, but I thought maybe it was because she had patients all morning. She's a dentist and has to work a lot.

"Oh, girls, you're here!" she said. "Alexis, how was your trip to the shore?"

"Actually, Mia's the one who went to beach," Alexis answered politely. "But thanks for asking."

Mom blushed. "Sorry, girls. I'm exhausted. My head feels like it's full of spaghetti today."

"That's okay, Mrs. Brown," Mia said. "I had a good time."

Then the phone rang. "That's probably your grandmother," Mom said to me. "Come find me if you need anything, okay?"

"Shmpf," I replied. Actually, I was saying "sure," but my mouth was full of guacamole.

Alexis took a chip and dipped it in the guacamole.

"Wow, that's really good," she remarked when she was done chewing. (Unlike me, Alexis doesn't ever talk with her mouth full.)

"Thanks," I said. "Guacamole is my new favorite food. I could eat it all day. Guacamole on pancakes, guacamole pizza for dinner . . ."

"Guacamole-and-jelly sandwiches for lunch," Mia said, giggling.

"Gross!" Emma squealed.

"I think I'll stick to guacamole and chips," Alexis said matter-of-factly.

Then she wiped her hands on a napkin and opened up her notebook. "Okay. So, I was looking at our client list," she began. Alexis loves to get down to business at a Cupcake Club meeting. "The only thing on our schedule this fall is our usual gig at The Special Day. We need to drum up some new business. I was thinking that we could send out a postcard to everyone who's ever ordered cupcakes from us. You know, something like 'Summer's Over, and Cupcake Season Has Started.'"

"I like it," I said. "Mia learned how to do computer art and stuff at camp this summer. Maybe you could write it and Mia could design it."

"That reminds me," Mia said, pointing to her shirt. "I designed this. I could make a T-shirt for each of us. I thought we could wear them when we go on jobs."

"Oh, it's so cute!" Emma said. "Could my shirt be pink?"

Mia shrugged. "I guess so. We could each have a different color shirt if we want. Unless you want it to be more like a uniform."

"Or we could expand our business and sell the T-shirts, too," Alexis said, sounding excited. "I bet we could find a site online where we could get the shirts made cheaply, and sell them for a profit."

Mia frowned a little bit. "I don't know, Alexis. I was thinking these should just be for us, you know? Special."

"But you want to be a fashion designer, don't you?" Alexis asked. "This could be the start of your business. Mia's Cupcake Clothing!"

Mia looked thoughtful, and I couldn't tell if she liked the idea or not. I decided to change the subject. If Mia decided she was interested, she'd bring up the idea again. Sometimes Alexis can get a little pushy when she wants the club to do something. Which is mostly good, because otherwise we'd never get anything done.

"Wow, I can't believe school is starting so soon." Then I said with a nod to Emma and Alexis, "Though what I really still can't believe is Sydney's singing routine at your day camp's talent show. It's in my nightmares."

When I first started middle school last year, Sydney Whitman made my life miserable. So I didn't feel bad about making fun of her—well, not *too* bad, anyway. My grandma Carole says that two wrongs don't make a right, and she's got a point.

"Oh my gosh, I can't believe I forgot to tell you!" Emma said. "I have big news. *Huge!* You guys are *not* going to believe this!"

"Tell us what?" I asked.

"It's about Sydney," Emma said. "Sydney's mom came in and returned a bunch of books and told my mom that they were moving—to California!"

"No WAY!" I cried, jumping out of my chair. "Are you serious?"

Emma nodded. "I'm pretty sure they moved already. Sydney's dad got transferred to some company in San Diego or something. Sydney's mom said they had to move immediately for Sydney to start school there on time."

I started jumping up and down and waving my hands in the air.

"Look out, everyone. Katie's doing her happy dance," Mia said.

"This is awesome! Amazing! Stupendous! Wonderful! Did I say awesome?" I cried. "No more Sydney! No more Popular Girls Club to ruin our lives!"

"Well, actually, I'm sure the PGC will continue," Alexis replied. "They've still got Maggie and Bella and Callie. I bet Callie will become their new leader."

I felt like a balloon that somebody just popped. One of the reasons Sydney made my life miserable last year was because she took my best friend Callie away from me. Yes, I know that nobody forced Callie to dump me and become a member of the PGC. But it was always easier to blame Sydney than to get mad at Callie. Callie and I have been friends since we were babies.

"So Callie didn't mention any of this to you?" Mia asked.

"No!" I said, feeling a little exasperated. "I mean, I barely talk to her anymore."

I know I shouldn't get so freaked out about Callie. If she hadn't dumped me, I probably never would have become friends with Mia, Emma, and Alexis. There would be no Cupcake Club. And something happened to Callie when she got into middle school. Sometimes she could be not so nice. So it was probably for the best that we weren't friends. We saw each other when our families got together, but that was about it.

Still, I must admit, there was a little part of me that hoped, now that Sydney was gone, that Callie would be friends with me again. I imagined her showing up at the front door.

Oh, Katie, I have treated you so badly, she would say. *Can I please join your Cupcake Club?*

Of course, I would say, trying to be the better person. *I forgive you, Callie.*

Then again, that would make things pretty confusing, because Mia was my best friend now, and I'm not sure how this would all work. Now *my* head felt like it was full of spaghetti. (Although

I would never say that out loud, because that is such a weird mom thing to say.)

"Earth to Katie," Mia said. "You there?"

I snapped myself out of my fantasy. "Sorry. I must be in a guacamole haze," I said, taking my seat. "Okay. Enough about the PGC. Let's get down to business."

Maybe Alexis had the right idea, after all.

A Little Sweet Talk!

There are 16 words in this puzzle, and they all have something to do with your four favorite Cupcake girls! Can you find them all?

(If you don't want to write in your book, make a copy of this page.)

WORD LIST: ACCESSORY, BLUSH, CAKE, FAIRY, FROSTING, GOOFY, HAIR, INVOICE, LOCKER, MAKEUP, PARTY, PROFIT, PRICE, REPUTATION, STYLISH, WIG

```
R  E  P  U  T  A  T  I  O  N
C  O  E  C  I  O  V  N  I  K
F  Z  P  R  I  C  E  D  F  G
A  B  S  T  Y  L  I  S  H  Y
I  W  L  Y  T  R  A  P  N  C
R  Z  I  U  G  O  O  F  Y  P
Y  G  I  W  S  C  A  K  E  R
L  J  L  L  M  H  A  I  R  O
M  A  K  E  U  P  I  S  H  F
R  E  K  C  O  L  O  M  E  I
A  C  C  E  S  S  O  R  Y  T
G  N  I  T  S  O  R  F  A  B
```

All Mixed Up!

The words below were used in *Alexis Cool as a Cupcake*.
Unscramble each word, and write the correctly spelled
words on the lines. Then write the circled letters in order,
on the lines at the bottom of the page.
You'll have the answer to a silly cupcake riddle.

(If you don't want to write in your book, make a copy of this page.)

UBSESSIN (_) _ _ _ _ _ _

KEACPUC _ _ _ _ _ _(_)

YEALD _ _ _(_)_

TORTU (_)_ _ _ _

WEO _(_)_

WHEENALLO (_)_ _ _ _ _ _ _ _

PEICRE _ _ _(_)_ _

DERAPA (_)_ _ _ _ _

FESSPROION (_)_ _ _ _ _ _ _ _ _

TUMECOS _ _ _ _ _ _(_)

DIEINGRENT _ _ _ _ _(_)_ _ _

RIDDLE: Why did the cupcakes think the cook was mean?
RIDDLE ANSWER: Because she _ _ _ _ the eggs
and _ _ _ _ _ _ _ the cream!

ANSWER KEY:

A Little Sweet Talk!

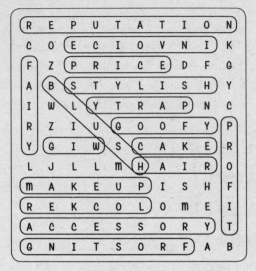

All Mixed Up!

UBSESSIN ⒷU S I N E S S

KEACPUC C U P C A K Ⓔ

YEALD D E L Ⓐ Y

TORTU ⓉU T O R

WEO O ⓌE

WHEENALLO ⒽA L L O W E E N

PEICRE R E C Ⓘ P E

DERAPA ⒫A R A D E

FESSPROION ⒫R O F E S S I O N

TUMECOS C O S T U M Ⓔ

DIEINGRENT I N G R E Ⓓ I E N T

RIDDLE: Why did the cupcakes think the cook was mean?
RIDDLE ANSWER: Because she B E A T the eggs
and W H I P P E D the cream!

Coco Simon always dreamed of opening a cupcake bakery but was afraid she would eat all of the profits. When she's not daydreaming about cupcakes, Coco edits children's books and has written close to one hundred books for children, tweens, and young adults, which is a lot less than the number of cupcakes she's eaten. Cupcake Diaries is the first time Coco has mixed her love of cupcakes with writing.

Still Hungry?
There's always room for another Cupcake! Make sure you've read them all!

Katie and the Cupcake Cure
978-1-4424-2275-9 $5.99
978-1-4424-2276-6 (eBook)

Mia in the Mix
978-1-4424-2277-3 $5.99
978-1-4424-2278-0 (eBook)

Emma on Thin Icing
978-1-4424-2279-7 $5.99
978-1-4424-2280-3 (eBook)

Alexis and the Perfect Recipe
978-1-4424-2901-7 $5.99
978-1-4424-2902-4 (eBook)

Katie, Batter Up!
978-1-4424-4611-3 $5.99
978-1-4424-4612-0 (eBook)

Mia's Baker's Dozen
978-1-4424-4613-7 $5.99
978-1-4424-4614-4 (eBook)

Emma All Stirred Up!
978-1-4424-5078-3 $5.99
978-1-4424-5079-0 (eBook)

Alexis Cool as a Cupcake
978-1-4424-5080-6 $5.99
978-1-4424-5081-3 (eBook)

Katie and the Cupcake War
978-1-4424-5373-9 $5.99
978-1-4424-5374-6 (eBook)

Did you **LOVE** this book?

Want to get access to
great books for **FREE?**

Join

where you can

✗ Read great books for FREE! ✗

• Get exclusive excerpts •

Chat with your friends

Vote on polls

Log on to **everloop.com**
and join the book loop group!

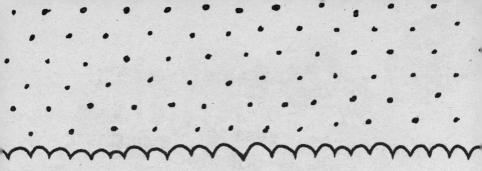

If you liked

CUPCAKE  DIARIES

be sure to check out these

other series from

Simon Spotlight

Sparkle Spa

Making friends one Sparkly nail at a time!